Romance Unbound Publishing

Obsession:
Girl Abducted

Previously titled: Stalked

Claire Thompson

Edited by Jae Ashley

Cover Art by Claire Thompson

ISBN: 979-8711963400

Chapter 1

Alana is naked in the white, empty room, her wrists strung high above her head, pulling her body taut. She lifts her head and whispers, "Mark. I love you. I've always loved you and only you."

"And I love you, Alana, my beloved. My slave girl."

Her legs are spread wide, held in place by a long bar of gleaming metal, attached cuffs securing each ankle. Her body is marked from the whip, each welt an offering. "I want to suffer for you, Sir," she says in her low, husky voice. "I was born to suffer for you."

"Yes," he agrees.

She drops her head again, her dark shiny hair tousled and damp with perspiration. He brings the whip down, striking her supple flesh again and again, coiling it around her thigh, her breasts, the perfect globes of her ass. Her cries echo in the empty room.

Mark lay on the bed, his hand on his cock as he watched her on the screen. Alana Hunter was laughing toward him, her dark blue eyes beckoning him as he sighed. He'd watched this video a dozen times or more, but he never tired of it. When the male character began to unbutton Alana's blouse, Mark moaned. *He* should be the only one to do that.

Soon he would be. Soon Alana Hunter, adored by millions, would belong to Mark and Mark alone. On the screen, Alana pouted at her faux lover, her lips like ripe fruit begging to be bitten. It wouldn't be long now, and Mark would be the only one to touch that lovely face, kiss those luscious lips, whip that perfect ass.

As Mark watched Alana surrender herself to her on-screen lover in the climactic final scene of the adventure-love story, longing dragged like a knife through his gut. He groaned as he pumped his cock, stroking in time to the movements of the lovers on the screen.

When she looked at the camera — at him — there was a sultry "I dare you" quality in her expression, but Mark knew she was an innocent. He'd followed her career for the past seven years with avid attention. Beyond the movies, he read every interview, scoured the internet for every story, feature and hint of gossip he could find, and wrote for several online blogs that catered to Alana Hunter fans.

Two years ago, he'd finally managed to get tickets to the screening of her latest movie, and that was the day he'd decided to stop living on the sidelines of Alana Hunter's life. Seeing her in person had been the most thrilling moment of his existence to that point.

She had worn a simple but elegant blue dress that clung alluringly to her perfect curves. She'd walked with the easy confidence of the beautiful and adored along the receiving line, stopping every few feet to be photographed and to greet her fans. When she'd turned her dazzling smile on Mark, electricity had sparked between them. Though she looked away a moment later to smile at the next fan, they'd shared something unique.

It was at that moment he began to devise his plan.

The credits were rolling across the screen and he still hadn't come. Closing his eyes, he let his favorite fantasy unfold once more…

Alana lifts her head, trying to focus those violet-blue eyes on her Master. Her breasts heave as she tries to catch her breath. "Thank you, Sir," she gasps.

"For what?" Mark demands.

"For whipping me, Sir. I needed it, Sir. I need you, Sir. Fuck me, my Master, my darling…"

Mark could almost feel Alana in the room with him, her perfect mouth wrapped around his cock. With a grunt, he exploded onto his stomach and chest. "Once I own you, Alana," he said aloud, "I'll have you lick me clean."

The autumn morning was crisp, a hint of snow in the air. Mark stood across the street from the studio where Alana Hunter was having her photo shoot for a women's fashion magazine. It should have been over by now. He glanced impatiently at his watch. He recognized her driver's car, a nondescript black sedan, its windows tinted to keep out prying eyes. It was parked near the back entrance of the studio on a narrow side street, ready to whisk away the woman of his dreams.

His heart leapt as the door opened and Alana came out, tossing her dark hair out of her face as she pulled her jacket more tightly around herself. She strode quickly toward the parked car. The passenger door was opened from inside, and she slipped in, shutting out any would-be autograph seekers or paparazzi before anyone even realized she was there.

Mark knew where she was going. It being

midday in Manhattan, he knew he would get there
as fast, if not faster, on foot.

Today she would be meeting with Lisa Carter,
her personal assistant, for lunch at Caliente, the
Mexican place on 6th Avenue in Greenwich
Village. After lunch, she would go for her massage
at Chez Paul, and then off to the studio to rehearse
or do whatever she did in there. So far, he hadn't
been able to get into that studio. The damn security
was too tight. He didn't care, though. What did it
matter?

He knew where she lived.

Mark Stratton knew as much about Alana
Hunter as anyone alive. He knew she had been
born in Galveston, Texas, and her parents still lived
in Houston. Her father was a doctor and her
mother was a writer and illustrator of children's
books. Her older sister lived in Dallas with two
children, a husband and three dogs.

She kept an apartment in the city, but spent
several months a year filming in Los Angeles,
where she owned a small house in Malibu. He had
seen all twelve movies she had been in, even the
first one, in which she had a bit part as the star's
little sister, and he had downloaded every
interview and YouTube video of her there was, not
to mention bought every magazine in which she'd

ever appeared.

She was slated soon to begin work on a romantic comedy, with that untalented pretty boy, Tim Rutherford, as her co-star. Despite all the bullshit gossip and speculation on Twitter and in the tabloids, Mark was certain they weren't romantically involved. No way Alana Hunter would stoop so low.

As he hurried along the crowded streets of New York, he almost tripped over a homeless guy who was snoring loudly, slumped against the wall of a building. Mark cursed softly under his breath as he stepped over the bum. He hated the city and his crappy, expensive, tiny apartment. Even in her snazzy penthouse, Alana probably hated it, too.

Happily, it was temporary. He was nearly ready to put his plan into action. At last he would save his darling girl from the undisciplined turmoil of public life. She would love the home he'd been working on every spare moment for the past year and a half.

Luckily, his job as a programmer with a software development company was going quite well. He had been slowly getting them used to the idea of his working less and less in the office, and more and more remotely. They were okay with this, for the most part, as long as the work got done. They recognized his creative genius, and thus gave him the leeway he needed, not to mention an excellent salary and a generous stock option plan.

He got to the restaurant just as Alana's driver was opening the car door for her. Mark's fists clenched in sudden rage, but it was just jealousy. The driver got to be close to Alana, so close he could smell her perfume. He got to take her places and open doors for her. Maybe they chatted as they drove, Alana telling him tidbits about her latest project.

Calming himself, Mark waited a minute or so in the shadows before entering the restaurant. Spying Alana and Lisa at a table near the back, he managed to get himself seated in a small booth nearby.

Poor Alana, she looked tired. She worked much too hard. Soon that burden would be lifted from her lovely shoulders. Soon, her sole occupation in life would be to be worshipped and adored by him, Mark Stratton, the only man who properly understood and appreciated her.

Sometimes he imagined them together as husband and wife, strolling in the park, a baby in Alana's arms. Alas, children weren't in her future. Mark had suffered an injury when he played college football, which had made him sterile. Just as well. He wouldn't want to share Alana with anyone else, not even their child. She would belong only to him, forever and always.

Mark's musings were shattered as he overheard Lisa's words. "Yes, he called again for you. *And* he sent a huge bouquet of the most beautiful flowers I've ever seen. The note said he can't wait to work with you, and that he's your biggest fan, and he signed it, 'with love and anticipation, Tim.'"

Tim! Rutherford, that bastard. How dare he push himself on Alana like that? The nauseating little prick.

"Wow, I can't wait to see the flowers. Tim is so hot I'm afraid I might get burned during our sex scenes," Alana replied with a grin, her eyes sparkling with amusement and mischief.

Blood rushed into Mark's face, every muscle in his body tensing for a fight. A lesser man might have leapt up at that moment to protest, but not Mark. Oh no, Mark was nothing if not patient. He had waited a long time for the right moment to introduce himself to his beloved. He wasn't about to blow that now, just because that pretty-boy asshole Rutherford thought he could charm Alana.

But he would have to move fast. Clearly, Alana

had deluded herself into thinking she wanted to work with this jerk, even to do love scenes with him. Mark couldn't bear the thought of her lying naked in another man's arms, even under the bright, artificial lights of a film studio. Another man's mouth on her perfect nipples. Another man's whip lashing that tender flesh…

She was scheduled to fly to Los Angeles soon. It would be too late to stop Rutherford from his attempts to corrupt the pure and lovely Alana. Since she had dumped that ridiculous low-life movie director last year, his Alana had remained faithful to Mark, telling the interviewers she was enjoying being single for now. She had saved that creamy flesh for his use alone.

Soon — very soon — she would belong to Mark, and dreams she didn't even know she had would be realized.

Two days later, he was ready to make his move. Even at this early hour, the city hummed and honked. The air was chilly, the sun still hidden behind the skyscrapers. Mark waited by Alana's apartment building, the black sedan car he'd bought in anticipation of this fateful day parked by the curb in front. It was an identical model to the ones driven by the studio chauffeurs.

Mark knew her routines, and Alana liked to come out a few minutes early, since it was usually impossible for her driver to find a parking spot. She would be waiting by the curb when he finally sidled up to retrieve her. Today, however, her *new* driver would be waiting for her. With a little digging and using his superior computer skills, it had been ridiculously easy to track down the name and pertinent information for her regular driver, and to send him a phone text that he was to pick up Alana at a different location that morning. He'd procured a nearly identical uniform to the one the studio drivers wore. Now it was just down to timing and good luck. Today was the day — the culmination of all his hard work and planning. Soon, she would be his.

He held his breath as the doorman opened the door and Alana appeared, radiant in a bright yellow cotton sweater and faded blue jeans, a brown leather jacket slung casually over her shoulder. From now on she would be wearing only dresses, if anything. He wanted to see those glorious legs at all times. And, of course, she must always be available to him.

As she walked toward the car, he pushed the passenger door open, hoping she didn't notice that his hand was trembling. "Good morning, Ms. Hunter," he said in a subdued but pleasant tone, though he could barely hear himself speak over the pounding of his heart.

"Oh." Alana looked at him uncertainly. "Hank isn't—?"

"Hank is sick," Mark said smoothly. "I'll be your driver just for the day, ma'am. My name is Mark. I'll drive you to the studio, Ms. Hunter."

She paused, still apparently uncertain, and for one horrible moment, he thought she was on to him. All his carefully laid plans would be ruined. She would refuse to get in and she would call the police.

Sweat prickled at his armpits as he forced a calm smile. "I'm sorry no one let you know, ma'am, but if you could get in? I'm not supposed to park here."

He almost sighed aloud with relief as she shrugged and nodded. "Okay. Thanks." She climbed into the back seat, and Mark began to breathe again.

He could smell her perfume, something light and slightly spicy. He could have reached back and touched her soft cheek then and there. He could touch that perfectly rounded breast. She was in his car. He had her.

He had her!

Loud, angry honking brought him back to the reality of New York City traffic. Smiling at her in the rearview mirror, he clicked the childproof locks into place and eased into the street. He began to weave his way through the early morning traffic.

Alana leaned back in the seat and closed her eyes.

Excellent. He would have that much longer until she began to notice that they weren't, in fact, going to the studio after all.

Several minutes later, as he was easing onto the George Washington Bridge, Alana opened her eyes and looked out the window. Her face creased into a frown. "Hey, where are you going? This isn't the way to the studio."

"Sorry," Mark said, affecting a bland air. "Didn't they tell you? We have to pick up another actor for the shoot."

Alana looked suspiciously at him, her eyes narrowing. The sweetest little furl appeared between her eyebrows. "Who?" she demanded. "I wasn't told about this."

"Marilee Bateman."

"Marilee?" Alana shook her head. "She's not even in the city right now." Her frown deepened.

"What's going on here?"

He hadn't known Marilee Bateman was out of town. Shit. Oh well, he'd just have to make his move that much sooner. It would be fine.

"Listen, Alana—" he began amiably.

"Alana? I'm Alana now? Take me to the studio this instant." She fumbled in her huge bag, no doubt reaching for her fucking cell phone. He could hear an edge of panic beneath her attempt to sound authoritative.

His cock responded to the sexy note of fear in her voice. He thrilled to the idea he could make his darling little girl afraid. And this was just the beginning. He would teach her real fear once he had her where he wanted her.

Before she could find her phone, he reached a hand into his jacket pocket and pulled out the gun he'd purchased just for her. Aiming it back toward her in a much-practiced gesture, he said, "Put your bag and jacket in the front seat. Don't try anything stupid."

"Oh, my god," she whispered, her eyes glued to the gun.

"Do as you're told," Mark said, his voice firm. "I'm not stealing your things, don't worry. I'll keep them safe for you. Hand them over and I'll explain everything." He waved his gun for emphasis, his eyes flickering between the road and the mirror.

"Who are you?" Alana asked, still whispering, but she handed her Louis Vuitton bag and leather jacket over the seat.

He reached into her bag and rummaged until his fingers closed over her cell phone. Pulling it free, he opened his window and dropped it onto the road, noting with satisfaction in the rearview mirror that it was immediately run over by the car behind him.

"Hey!" Alana cried. "What the hell? That was my phone!"

"Relax. You won't be needing it anymore. I am your savior, Alana. I'm taking you away from the strife and chaos of your life. We're going to a safe haven where we can get to know each other, without all those agents, producers, directors and paparazzi harassing you every hour of the day and night. I am setting you free, my love."

He looked triumphantly in the mirror as he waited for her response. Naturally, she wouldn't understand yet, but in time, she would appreciate what he'd done for her — for them. At the moment, however, she looked horrified — there was no other word for it.

"Don't worry, darling," he soothed. Oh, it felt delicious to say that! "I won't use this" — again he pointed the gun again at her — "unless, of course, you make me."

She made a small whimpering sound that went directly to his cock.

Glancing from the road to her face in the mirror, he continued, "I'm Mark, as I told you earlier. You don't know me, but I know you. I'm your biggest fan."

I really am her biggest fan. Not like that asshole Rutherford who just wants to get into her pants.

"I've seen all your work," he went on, smiling. "Even that dreadful shampoo commercial you did back in the early days of your career. I know where you live. I know your daily schedule. I know where you eat. I know who your friends are. I know who your family is and where they live and what they all do for a living."

As Mark spoke, Alana looked more and more frightened. This irritated him. She ought to be flattered to know he was so interested in her and her life.

"A stalker!" she blurted. "You're a stalker, oh

my god, oh my god." Her normally husky voice rose, ending on a squeak.

"No name calling, little girl," he replied, stung by the unfair term. They were over the bridge now, heading northwest. "Just pretend you're Catherine in *The China Hunt*. I'll be Garth Blackstone." It hadn't been one of her more famous films, but Mark loved it. It was romantic, but more importantly, she got kidnapped and tied to a chair. There was an implied whipping, though the audience didn't get to see it. Her screams in the film had been heart-wrenchingly real. He had watched that scene so many times there wasn't a detail that escaped him.

He glanced back at Alana, amused by her look of confused fear as she took in what he'd just said. After all, Garth Blackstone hadn't been the "good guy." He was the abductor who had plans to murder Catherine if his demands weren't met.

Alana began to cry quietly, large tears welling and spilling over. "Please, don't hurt me," she begged sweetly. "Please, take me back home. Please."

Again his cock fought with him, straining against the fabric of his polyester uniform. He loved the terror in her eyes and the way her voice cracked with fear and pleading. But he also loved

Alana, and didn't want her to suffer too much. At least not like this. Not yet.

"I am taking you home, darling. To our home. I've been working and saving for two years for this. I have it all arranged so I can work from home. I'll never leave you alone again, my beloved. No more lonely nights for you. No more endless work schedules with all those vultures profiting off your talents."

Alana continued to cry, her head now hidden in her hands. Mark was annoyed. Wasn't she listening to him? "Stop it at once. I don't like that crying. I just gave you wonderful news."

Twisting back for a second, he touched the top of her bowed head with the hard metal of the gun.

Alana jumped and jerked her head back with a cry.

Again facing forward, Mark glanced angrily into the rearview mirror. "Your face is a mess. I told you to stop that damn crying." She was ruining her pretty face with the mascara-streaked tears and the ugly expression. He'd have to focus on something else. A brilliant idea popped into his head. After all, the windows were tinted — no one could see in. "Take off that sweater," he commanded. "And your bra too."

Mark's cock swelled painfully at the realization he was about to see her breasts for the first time — the first time in real life, that was. She'd bared them for the world in *Heart Thief*, but only because the producers demanded an R rating.

"What?" Alana said stupidly, though at least she'd stopped crying. She wiped a hand across her nose and his heart almost burst with tenderness. She looked like a little girl who had fallen and skinned her knee. But the little girl was being naughty. He had given her a specific order.

"Alana, what did I tell you?" He couldn't quite believe he was talking to the woman of his dreams like this. He couldn't believe his own wonderful, masterful nerve as he commanded her to obey him. "I said take off that sweater and bra. *Now*." He cocked the hammer of the gun to emphasize his point.

With a small, sexy gasp, Alana lifted the hem of her sweater and began to pull it up over her head. Mark almost swerved into a guardrail as her bra-encased breasts were revealed.

"Go on," Mark said in a low voice, not trusting himself to say more. His heart was pounding so hard his chest actually hurt.

Averting her face, Alana reached behind her

back and unclasped the lacy black bra. As her breasts popped into view in his mirror, Mark had trouble keeping his eyes on the road. He would have pulled over but he didn't want to attract any unwelcome attention.

The pink blush that had started on her face was creeping down her neck and torso. "Come on," he teased, hugely enjoying her sweet shyness. "It's not like you haven't bared those delicious breasts of yours to the entire world. Lift up your head and throw back your shoulders. Be proud, girl!"

She lifted her head with obvious reluctance. Her lovely breasts swelled from her body like soft round peaches. The creamy skin was tipped with dark pink nipples. Mark's mouth literally watered at the thought of tasting those perfect mounds of feminine perfection.

"Squeeze your nipples for me," he ordered, nearly drunk on his newfound power. "Make them hard."

When she didn't immediately obey, Mark waved the gun, and her fingers flew to her nipples. She twisted and rolled the soft pink flesh until the nubbins were as hard as marbles. Mark had to struggle to keep his car between the lines, but he couldn't resist glancing back repeatedly at his captive.

"Put your hands behind your head, like in *Heart Thief.*"

Again looking away, her lower lip caught in her teeth, Alana obeyed.

"Ah," Mark breathed. He could touch her if he wanted. She was that close to him. He stared at her in the mirror as he maneuvered through the traffic. He longed to reach back and twist her lovely, erect nipples, but he didn't dare. He didn't want to embarrass himself by coming in his pants. Plenty of time to touch her later.

Turning back in his seat, Mark directed, "Keep your arms that way for a while, Alana. I like the way it looks." He continued down the highway, his eyes darting from the road to his mirror as often as possible.

Mark was no stranger to exerting his dominant sexual will with submissive girls, but up until now the exchange of power had been mostly consensual. Over the years he had cruised the BDSM clubs in the city, easily finding masochistic sluts eager to play with him. If they were attractive enough, he would take them to a hotel or let them take him back to their apartment, where he would whip and tease them until they were begging to be fucked.

Sometimes he'd agree to see them again, but not often. For these women, the experience had been a game. They "let" him tie them down and spank them. They "let" him sexually humiliate them, simpering as they called him Master. After a day, a week, a month, he invariably became bored and sent them packing.

As he pondered his rather lackluster experience as a Dom, he understood that the missing ingredient was love. Without passion, there could be no poetry. Without love, the intensity of a true exchange of power was diminished. Mark knew in his bones this time it would be different — because this time he would have his Alana.

An hour later found them in the countryside of the Lower Hudson Valley. Mark maneuvered the car along an unpaved lane that dead-ended into a converted farmhouse. "We're home." He grinned in the rearview mirror at Alana, who was still half-naked and now hunched into a corner of the back seat.

After their initial exchange, she hadn't said a word during the whole trip, save for the monosyllabic responses he occasionally forced from her. After a while, they had simply driven in silence.

"Put on your jacket." He tossed it back to her.

"There's no one around here, but I don't even want those horses to see you. You're all mine now."

Alana reached for her sweater and bra.

"No." Mark corrected her actions. "Nothing else. Just the jacket."

Alana pulled on the jacket over her slender, bare torso.

He climbed out of the car and opened her door, his gun aimed at her as she exited the vehicle. Stepping behind her, he pressed the gun against the small of her back as he propelled her toward the front door.

Using the keypad he'd had installed beneath the lock, he punched in the code to release the deadbolt with his free hand. Opening the door, he gestured Alana over the threshold.

"Welcome to your new home. What do you think?" He beamed at her as she looked around the large room that was comfortably furnished with overstuffed chairs and a couch set in a semi-circle around a huge old stone fireplace, a large rectangular wooden table and chairs set up to serve for their more formal dining area. Mark was immensely proud of this room, which he had spent many weekends restoring, furnishing and decorating.

"Well?" he demanded, a little irritated at her lack of response.

Alana glanced down at the gun and up at his face. "It's very nice," she said in her trademark, slightly husky, incredibly sexy voice. "Is it yours?"

"It's ours, Alana. Ours."

Alana didn't respond.

Frustrated, he grabbed her arm and pulled her through the space and along the narrow hallway. "This is our bedroom," he said as he led her into the master bedroom, which was almost completely filled by a four-poster bed of dark pinewood, heaped with beautiful, handmade patchwork quilts. He had hung two whips over the bed, crossed in an X over a large ringbolt secured firmly into the wall.

"Those are for you, sweetheart," Mark informed Alana as she stared at the wall. "And wait till you see the dungeon playroom."

"The…what?" she said faintly.

Taking her arm again, Mark dragged Alana farther down the hall. He turned the large key in the lock on the last door and opened it. Turning on the light, he pushed Alana gently into the room.

Her eyes grew rounder, her mouth falling open as she clasped her hands over her heart. "Jesus," she breathed, obviously impressed.

The room was white, stark white. Even the wooden floor was painted white, just like in his favorite fantasy. A vast array of whips, riding crops, chains, handcuffs, spreader bars, ropes and ball gags hung along one wall. Across from them sat a large wooden chair with cuffs built into the legs and armrests. There was a padded bar, perfect for bending a naked slave over. A thick metal rod hung parallel to the floor from a large pulley he'd affixed in the ceiling, chains dangling with cuffs at their ends. A St. Andrew's cross waited for his captive, its leather restraints ready.

Mark turned to regale his beloved with all the wonderful, terrible things he planned to do to her in this room, but before he could get out a word, her eyes slid upward in her head as the color drained away from her face. Instinctively, he reached out to catch her as she slumped toward the floor.

Chapter 2

Alana awoke with a start, her mind muddled. It took her several seconds to get her bearings. She was in a bed, her head resting on a mound of soft feather pillows. When she tried to sit up, she realized her wrists and ankles were bound in thick black leather cuffs. She saw with horror that she was naked, and she let out a mewl of terror. Her legs were chained together, her wrists attached to a long chain that lay loose on the bed, its other end secured to a ringbolt in the wall behind her. The terrifying events of the past few hours, if that was how long it had been, crowded in on her like a dark, thick fog.

"Oh god, help me," she pleaded into the air.

"I'll help you, dearest girl."

Alana jumped and whipped her head in the direction of the voice.

The madman who had abducted her was sitting on a chair in the corner of the room, his eyes fixed on her. He had changed from the driver's uniform into faded blue jeans and a black T-shirt. He was actually quite good looking, and the thought somehow didn't compute. How could someone so handsome be such a raving lunatic?

"You belong to me, Alana," he said in a conversational tone, as if they were friends, his lips lifting into a friendly smile. "I know you aren't very happy about it at the moment, but hopefully you will come to realize I've actually rescued you."

Rescued her? From what? "Let me go," Alana demanded furiously. "You can't possibly think you'll get away with this. People know me."

"Ah, but they don't know me. No one in New York knows me, except the people I work for, and as far as they know, I will now be working entirely from my country home. There's nothing to tie you and me together. Nothing of mine is left in the city. I have vanished. And so, my love, have you."

"Why are you doing this? Are you crazy?" She could hear her voice edging toward hysteria, her heart beating like a wild bird in her chest. Even as she asked this, she knew it was a pointless question. He was a stalker, and she'd had them before, though nothing like this. They were mostly social media stalkers, and guys who hung around the back entrance to movie studios and photo shoots, hoping for a glimpse, wilted bouquets in their hands, a lovesick look on their faces. A stern talking-to by one of the studio tough guys, and, on one occasion, a visit from the local police, had been enough to make them back off. But this guy was in a totally different category. He seemed to actually believe the crazy shit he was spouting.

"Crazy in love, maybe." He smiled as if he'd said something witty. "My love for you is very special, as you are about to learn. You see, I like control. Total and complete control." His smile edged into something cruel that sent an arrow of dread directly into Alana's gut. "You don't yet understand. But you will."

Terror rose into Alana's throat, escaping her mouth in a scream.

The madman who had called himself Mark rose to his feet and moved close to the bed, looming over her. "Shut up. Stop it," he yelled, but she couldn't have stopped, even if she'd wanted to. He pulled back his hand and slapped her across the face.

After a sharp, stunned intake of breath, Alana just screamed louder.

"All right, then," Mark said, his mouth a thin line of determination. "If that's how you want to start out. I was saving this for later, but if you insist." He marched out of the room and returned a moment later with a bright red ball gag in his hand. Leaning over her, he pressed the disgusting rubber ball between her lips, forcing her tongue back and stifling her cries. As he reached out to buckle the strap behind her head, Alana tried ineffectually to twist away.

He grabbed the chain that held her wrists and yanked it up, winding it through the ringbolt and forcing Alana's arms up and back over her head in the process. He then reached for the chain between her ankles and pulled it up and over her body, also attaching it to the ringbolt. This forced Alana's legs up into the air, as if she were in a hospital bed, immobilized after a ski accident.

She thrashed wildly in her chains, but to no avail. Saliva pooled in her mouth and dripped around the ball as she squirmed and whimpered, but the deranged man only stared down at her with a nasty smile.

~*~

She looked so incredibly beautiful, so helpless in her bonds. Mark stood for a long moment, drinking in the sight of his naked prisoner, bound and pulled taut by her chains. Now that he actually had her just where he wanted her, he had no idea where to start. Should he whip her first? Or lovingly melt hot wax onto those perfect breasts, letting the hot liquid splash here and there, finally searing her nipples with its fire?

His cock was straining hard against his jeans. Reaching down, he unzipped his pants. Yes. He would make love to her first. Claim her in that traditional manner before he set about claiming her soul.

"Alana." His voice was hoarse with barely controlled lust. She stared at him, her dark blue eyes wide over the gag. "I can't decide whether to whip you or fuck you."

Her eyes fluttered shut and her head fell back. She had fainted again.

Mark moved closer to the nude, bound woman. Bending over her slack body, he carefully released and removed the ball gag from her mouth and gently wiped the drool from her chin. He released the cuffs and chains that held her legs, and they flopped back down onto the bed.

"Alana," he said softly. "Come back to me."

Alana's eyes slowly opened.

"Welcome back." Mark said with a smile. "You weren't out so long this time. You really need to stop passing out. It's annoying. I might lose my patience and throw a bucket of cold water on you next time."

"Please let me out of these chains," she begged in a sweet, trembling voice. "My arms hurt. My wrists, too. Please, Mark. Please."

She'd said his name. A shiver of pleasure rushed through Mark's psyche. "If I let you out, will you be a good girl, darling? No more screaming? And you won't try anything stupid like trying to run away, will you? I'd hate to have to shoot you." He touched the gun, which he'd tucked into the front waistband of his jeans. It was unloaded, of course, but she didn't know that.

Her eyes widened with fear as they followed his hand, and he could see her visibly swallow. "Yes, Mark," she said, her voice cracking. "I promise."

This was excellent. She was coming around nicely, and Mark's spirits soared. Reaching up, he unhooked the chain that held her arms suspended and removed the thick leather cuffs. Perching on the bed beside her, he said, "I'm glad you're coming to accept your new situation. We'll start out simple. There are rules in my house, and you'll come to learn them all. The first one is this."

He opened the drawer in the nightstand and

took out four iron bracelets. He'd had them custom-made just for her and he couldn't wait to put them on. Each bracelet had a clasp comprised of two small ovals, an O-ring welded in place on the opposite side. When he snapped the clasps into place, they would be impossible to open without the aid of a special key. "Hold out your wrists," he instructed.

With another fearful glance at the gun, Alana did as she was told, and he clicked the bracelets into place, first on her wrists, then on her ankles. The fit was perfect and she looked breathtakingly lovely in his jewelry. "These slave bracelets symbolize your servitude and my ownership of you," he informed her with a satisfied smile. "In return for your absolute obedience and submission, I promise to cherish and adore you."

Her expression was either one of horror or fear. Mark decided on the latter. "It's all right to be afraid, my sweet girl." He grasped her nipple and twisted, and she yelped in pain as she tried to shrink back from him. Letting her go, he stood and pulled the gun from his jeans.

"No, please," she cried. "Don't kill me!" She covered her face with her hands.

Mark laughed indulgently. "I'm not going to kill you, silly girl." His cock throbbed. He could hardly believe he'd exercised as much restraint as he had to this point, but he'd wanted her conscious for their first time. "I'm going to fuck you."

Ignoring the look on her face, he set the gun down on the nightstand and quickly pulled off his clothes, his eyes on her the whole time in case she got any stupid ideas.

Naked, he draped himself over his darling Alana. When she yelped, he clamped his hand over her mouth. Using his knee, he easily forced her thighs apart. His rock-hard cock pressed against her pussy. She wasn't properly wet, but he wouldn't punish her just yet for that. Instead, he spit onto his fingers and coated the head of his cock with his saliva. Then, with one perfect thrust, he pushed himself inside.

Alana screamed against his hand, but that just made him harder. At the same time, the hot, velvet walls of her cunt contracted around his cock as he eased out and slammed back in. She wanted him! He desperately wanted to hold on, but it was too astoundingly fabulous to be buried inside his true love's pussy, and he came within seconds of penetration.

He slumped against her, breathing in the scent of her perfume mingled with the acrid, arousing scent of fear. Finally lifting himself onto his elbows, he looked at her. Her face was averted, her eyes squeezed tightly shut.

Grasping her by the chin, Mark forced her face toward his. "Open your eyes." When Alana didn't obey at once, he slapped her cheek lightly, just to get her attention. "I said, open your eyes."

She obeyed, and he saw the flash of fiery fury in her eyes. Not to worry — he would soon beat that out of her.

"Thank me," he ordered. He needed to be stern so she would understand her position. "You must always thank your Master for fucking you."

When she didn't respond, he lifted his hand again to strike her.

"Thank you," she said quickly.

"Thank you, Sir," he corrected.

"Thank you, Sir," she repeated somewhat mechanically, but he would take it, for now.

"You're welcome, my love. Now we'll have some lunch."

Alana hadn't eaten much during lunch, but Mark didn't worry overmuch. She would eat when she was hungry enough. He had pulled on his jeans, but hadn't allowed Alana to dress for the meal. It had been hard to focus on his food with the naked goddess kneeling on her cushion beside his chair.

Now he led her back to the bedroom. Sitting on the bed, he patted his thighs. She stood, naked and perfect in front of him. "You were a very naughty girl earlier, Alana, and now you will be punished. But since you're not yet properly trained, I'm just going to spank you — nothing too severe."

"What?" she squeaked.

"You heard me." He glanced meaningfully at the gun on the nightstand and then back at her.

Following his gaze, after a moment, she draped herself tentatively across his lap. Mark sighed with pleasure as he stroked and cupped her sexy ass.

Placing one hand on the small of her back, he smacked her right buttock, not too hard. She jumped. "Stay still," he admonished. He smacked the other side, harder this time, and Alana yelped. Her cry excited him and Mark began to spank her in earnest, until her skin grew hot beneath his palm. Her steady whimpering only served to turn his cock to steel, but when she started to struggle in an attempt to twist away, he began to get annoyed.

"I said stay still," he said sternly.

"You're hurting me. Please, stop. You're hurting me," she cried.

"You're being punished, Alana. Of course it hurts." He grabbed her wrists in one hand and pulled them out straight in front of her and smacked her hard with his cupped palm. She continued to wriggle and squirm, and finally, exasperated, he stood abruptly, letting her tumble to the floor.

Before she could get her bearings, he hauled her up by the arm and flipped her around, catching her wrists behind her, against his body. Marching her forward, he propelled her out of the room and down the hall. Clearly, this girl needed to be taught a lesson, and the sooner the better.

"Let me go. You bastard, let me go," she screamed.

Ignoring her cries, he pushed her into the playroom and spun her around so she was facing him. Even though she was behaving like a willful brat, he couldn't resist wrapping his arms around her and leaning down to kiss those luscious, full lips.

As he kissed her, Alana tried to pummel his

chest with her clenched fists, but she was no match for his vastly superior strength. With a laugh, Mark turned her around, again catching her arms and twisting them up behind her back until she gasped with pain.

He pushed her along to the St. Andrew's cross and lifted her onto the small platform so she was facing the cross. He raised her arms high and secured the O-rings in her wrist bracelets to clips attached to the cross. Crouching in front of her, he forced her legs apart and clipped her ankles to the legs of the cross. All the while she squealed and cursed him, between terrified whimpers and pleas for him not to kill her.

"Shut up," he finally ordered, her noise irksome. Hadn't he assured her he would cherish and adore her? But she seemed unable or unwilling to obey, still crying and begging as if he were about to chop off her head or something. It was too much, so he retrieved a ball gag from the supply cabinet and shoved it into her mouth, instantly muffling her annoying protests.

"Much better," he said, giving her still-reddened ass a swat for emphasis. "I was going to go easy on you this first time, but your flagrant disobedience calls for tougher measures." She tried to twist her head back to catch his eye, but he only shook his head. "No, no. You've only yourself to blame, Alana. I told you to be still, and you ignored me. I told you to be quiet, and you continued to squeal like a stuck pig. Now you're going to pay."

In spite of his threats, he decided to start with the flogger. After all, his darling girl was a complete novice when it came to BDSM play, and he was a responsible Dom. He chose a large flogger from the wall and brought it to the bound woman, holding it up for her to see.

Alana's face was turned sideways, and as she looked at the flogger, her eyes widened with fear, sending a jolt directly to his already erect cock. Moving closer, he reached between her legs and stroked her delicate pussy. He frowned — she wasn't properly wet for him. Didn't she know a slave girl must always be wet and ready for her Master?

No, he reminded himself. *She doesn't know. Not yet.*

But she would learn.

He would teach her.

Meanwhile, he knew how to arouse a woman. Licking his finger, he slid it gently into that delicious cunt and moved it slowly, sensually, inside her. After a moment, he withdrew it. Licking it once more, he rubbed lightly around her hooded clit, moving closer and closer to the hidden nubbin. He stroked and teased her for a minute or two, then pushed his finger once more gently inside her. This time her vaginal muscles clamped down on his finger, sending another jolt of electricity directly to his aching cock.

Keeping his desire under control, he teased the bound and helpless woman for several more minutes, alternating between frigging her cunt and rubbing and pinching her clit until she was wet and swollen, her muffled cries behind the ball gag stilled at last as she breathed heavily through her nose.

Now she was ready for the flogger. Nearly forgetting it was supposed to be a punishment, he whispered into her ear, "I'm going to flog you now, beautiful girl. I'm going to take you to heights you've never dreamed of."

She jumped at his words and started to whimper again against the ball gag. Mark decided to take it off—he wanted to hear her scream. Once he unbuckled and removed the gag, Alana at once begged him to let her go. Mark silenced her by reminding her he had a gun.

The threat worked, and she quieted. Mark

pulled off his jeans and brushed the soft leather strands of the flogger over his erect penis and then swished them lightly over Alana's perfect ass.

Alana jerked, but then stilled when she realized he wasn't hurting her. No — he was caressing her with the leather, warming and readying the skin for what was to come. For several minutes he simply stroked her flesh with the flogger, enjoying the sound of the leather brushing against her soft skin, and the contrast of the black whip against her pale flesh.

Alana's breathing slowed to something nearer to normal and she relaxed somewhat in her restraints. When he let the first real stinging blow land on the fleshiest part of her bottom, she flinched and yelped.

"There now," Mark crooned, barely able to contain his excitement. "That wasn't so bad, now was it?" He brought the flogger down again, even harder, across her ass. Then he whipped it in stinging strokes over her back and shoulders.

Alana cried out and jerked against her restraints, but this only spurred him on. "You know you want it, Alana. In your heart of hearts, you share every woman's fantasy of being kidnapped, raped and ravaged. You're just so incredibly lucky I'm the one to claim you, because I will cherish you as you deserve."

God, was he really saying this directly to the girl of his dreams? Was Alana Hunter actually naked and bound in his dungeon, suffering beneath his flogger? He could hardly believe it was real. Stunned at his astonishing good fortune, his cock hard as steel, he flogged Alana in earnest from shoulder to thigh. Her skin reddened beneath the stinging leather, her breathing ragged as she cried out with each stroke against her virgin flesh.

Only when his arm was tired did Mark finally drop the flogger. He draped his naked body against hers, his cock pressed just above her ass. He would have to make her wear high heels next time, so his cock could nestle right into the crack of those perfect globes.

Taking a step back, he released Alana from the cross and caught her as she fell back. Lifting her into his arms, he settled her onto the floor in front of him and pulled her up so she was on her knees. Just to be safe in case she got any stupid ideas, and because he liked the way it looked, he clipped her slave bracelets together behind her back. Returning to gaze down at her, he smoothed tendrils of her hair from her tear-stained cheeks and tucked them behind her ears.

"You did very well for your first time," he

informed her. She stared up at him, mute. Slightly annoyed that she'd ignored his compliment, he prompted, "When I praise you, you will thank me."

A flash of fury moved over her face, but she quelled it before he was forced to slap her for her impudence, and instead said, if somewhat stiffly, "Thank you."

"Thank you…?" he trailed off, adding, "What did you forget? Thank you…?"

"Thank you, Sir," she muttered.

He smiled. His cock was still hard, and his balls ached. Gripping his shaft, he moved the head close to her mouth. "Straighten up. I'm going to let you worship my cock as proof of your thanks."

She didn't move.

He grabbed her head with both hands and forced her face down onto his cock. He moved forward slowly, not stopping until he had slid his cock down her throat.

Gagging, Alana tried to pull back, but Mark wasn't about to let her. She had probably sucked off that bastard Rutherford, or was planning to, when they met up for the movie shoot. Well, the movie was off. All bets were off now. She had a new job — a new vocation — serving him and him alone.

Her lips and tongue felt good on his shaft, the muscles in her throat yielding to his onslaught. He held her head in place as he thrust in and out of her lovely mouth, holding himself back to sustain his pleasure. Yet, all too soon, he felt that delicious tightening sensation in his balls. Overcome, he spurted his seed in a series of jolts down her open throat. He held her close, her face mashed against his pubic bone, until he was spent.

When he finally let her go, Alana fell back onto the floor, coughing and gasping. Mark pulled her to her feet and lifted her into his strong arms. He carried her down the hall and into the bedroom, passing through to the bathroom, where he set her gently on her knees on the bath rug in front of the sink. She had a dazed look on her face, which was understandable, as she'd been through a lot her first day as his sex slave.

He ran the water until it was warm, then wet a washcloth, which he used to gently wipe away the remains of her makeup. She didn't need all that glop—her skin was perfection itself.

Since they were in the bathroom, he thought to ask, "Do you need to pee, Alana?" Even as he asked, he knew she must have to. She hadn't used the toilet since he'd first abducted her hours before.

He quite liked the idea of making her pee in front of him. A proper slave held nothing back from her Master. To his surprise, however, she shook her head.

"That won't do," he informed her. "You'd better have something to drink then." He leaned down and gripped her shoulders, forcing her to her feet. Stopping in the bedroom, he pulled on a pair of jeans, slipping the gun into his waistband for good measure.

In the kitchen, he opened the refrigerator and removed a bottle of champagne. He popped the cork. "To us." He poured them each a large goblet of the bubbly wine.

She eyed the glass and lifted her shoulders. "Please, can you release my wrists? I can't drink to your toast if my arms are bound."

"Of course you can. I'll hold the glass for you." He lifted the wineglass to her lips and tipped it carefully.

She took a swallow, and when he tilted it, she sipped some more. He continued to let her drink until she'd drained the glass. Courage in a bottle?

"Please, Mark," she entreated. "It's not too late. Please let me go. I won't press charges, I promise.

Just let me go. Let me call a cab, drive me somewhere and leave me, whatever you want. I'm begging you." Her voice cracked. "Please let me go."

Mark shook his head. "You silly girl, why would I do that? We're meant to be together, you and I. It's fate. Now" — he took hold of her arm — "I'm going to watch you urinate."

"What?" she blurted, apparently confused.

"That's right," he said with a smile as he propelled her toward the master bathroom once more. "I knew you had to pee before, but I decided to give you champagne to help you relax. It's not so much that I want to watch you pee, but more the power implied in the action, you see. I want you to understand that I have taken control of every aspect of your existence, including your bodily functions. From now on, you will ask me for permission to use the toilet and I may or may not allow you to do so, depending on my mood, and if you've been a good girl that day."

"This is nuts," she dared to protest. "You can't make me do this."

"I can make you do whatever I like, Alana," Mark snapped, trying to keep his temper under control. After all, she still didn't fully understand her situation. "I own you." He dragged her into the bathroom and pushed her toward the toilet.

As he forced her to sit, she shouted, "No, this is insane. Let me go!"

His anger spilled over and he slapped her face, the impact of his blow whipping her head to the side. "Let's get something straight right now," he said, gritting his teeth to keep from shouting. "You are never, I repeat, *never*, to say the word 'no' to me. I know you aren't used to me yet, and you aren't used to my expectations. But get it through your head, Alana. This is not a negotiation. You don't have options. You don't have the right to refuse. If I hear 'no' from you again, I'll punish you severely. Are we crystal clear on this?"

Alana didn't answer. But she didn't protest either. Her cheek was red where he'd struck her, and there were tears in her beautiful eyes. His cock stirred, but he ignored it.

"Now do what you've been told. Your bladder has to be full to bursting. Do I have to shoot you?"

"No," she whispered. Averting her head, she finally began to pee into the bowl, a trickle at first and then a steady stream.

When she was done, he crouched in front of her

and gently wiped between her legs, his heart aching with tenderness. "That wasn't so hard, was it?"

She didn't reply, but again he let it go. He would teach her proper slave protocol. They had plenty of time—all the time in the world.

Chapter 3

Sunlight was streaming through the window as Mark opened his eyes. He yawned and stretched. Alana, curled at the foot of his bed beneath the sheets, moaned softly in her sleep. As memories of their first night together flooded through his mind, Mark prodded the still sleeping young woman with his toe.

He had done it. He'd abducted the girl of his dreams, and now he would be all the reality she ever needed. Today they would begin her training in earnest. His cock hardened with anticipation. "Alana, wake up. My cock needs attention."

Alana began to whimper. "Help me. Someone, help me," she mumbled. She began to thrash beneath the sheets, the chain that secured her to the headboard snaking beside him on the bed.

"Hush, Alana. You're dreaming. It's okay. Wake

up. Wake up." He pulled her up next to him but instead of calming down, she stiffened, pushing against him with shackled wrists, the chain hitting against his chest.

"Help me, help me," she continued to moan, apparently not yet fully awake.

Mark grabbed her wrists and held them tight. Her eyes flew open and she stared at him. "Oh my god," she whispered. "This can't be real. This can't be happening."

Mark shook his head and pulled her tighter into his arms. "Hush, now. You're upsetting yourself needlessly. You're safe. You have been set free from the world that feeds off your fame and talent. Your only focus now will be learning to serve me. I am your Master. I own you."

Alana went limp in his arms, but when he shifted to see her face, it was twisted into an ugly grimace. "You won't get away with this," she hissed.

"I already have," he replied calmly. "The deed is done. And now it's time for you to accept it and deal with it."

Alana turned her head away, the anger fairly radiating from her form. He was getting annoyed again. He'd been tolerant because of the initial shock, but enough was enough.

He grabbed her by the hair and forced her to turn back toward him. "I know you hate me right now and that's regrettable. But I adore you. I've waited a lifetime for you. I will never, ever, let you go."

Alana didn't speak. She had closed her eyes, as if she could escape in some small measure by refusing to look at him. Mark decided to let this pass. His cock was rigid, pressed hard against her thigh. "Now, I want you to suck my cock. Do it like your life depends on it. Because guess what? It does."

He pushed her down and forced her head to his cock. Her lips were pressed tightly closed, but a swift slap across her face caused her to gasp, and when her pretty mouth opened, he shoved his erect cock between her lips.

A sudden, sharp pain circled his shaft like needles, and he shouted with surprised pain as he instinctively shoved her away. "You bit me, you fucking cunt!" Blind fury scalded his brain, and without stopping to think, he smacked Alana hard across the back of her head, the force of his blow knocking her from the bed.

She scrambled to her feet as if to run, but Mark jumped up, easily catching up to her with one long stride. Grabbing her by the throat, he swung her back toward the bed. Pinning her with his own body, he sat across her chest. Alana kicked and thrashed, desperately trying to free herself from his grasp.

He sat back slightly, straddling her hips, his cock resting lightly on her belly. While she continued to struggle helplessly beneath him, Mark looked down at his bruised shaft. She hadn't broken the skin. Lucky for her. Still, this continued, willful defiance was unacceptable.

"I can see that you need to be punished. You obviously don't yet understand your position. I'm going to teach you how to behave, little girl. The lesson starts now and will go on for as long as it takes."

Climbing off her, Mark stood and pulled his captive roughly to her feet.

Alana continued to struggle, ineffectually batting at Mark's chest with her fists. "Let me go! Let me go! Let me go!"

Ignoring her cries, Mark half-pushed, half-carried her toward the double doors of the large walk-in bedroom closet. Pulling open the doors, he thrust her into the closet. The space held clothing along one wall, his and hers, neatly hanging on two bars. Shoes were arranged in pairs on the cedar floor beneath the clothing.

A large metal animal cage he'd purchased just for her stood against the other wall, its door open. Mark forced Alana into a crouching position and began to maneuver her into the cage. All at once, she reached up wildly and raked her fingernails down his cheek, leaving stinging trails in their wake. Mark barely noticed, intent on getting her into the cage.

Finally, he succeeded in forcing her into the enclosed space. He slammed the door shut with a clang and snapped the padlock into place.

"Let me go, you bastard, you bastard!" she howled.

As he regarded her, Mark touched his cheek, pulling back fingers smeared with his own blood. She certainly had spirit—he had to give her that. But then, that was one of the things he loved about her. Still, the feisty little bitch would have to pay. She had earned her punishment, and then some.

He walked out of the closet and closed the doors behind him without a backward glance. She continued to wail as he went into the bathroom to use the toilet and wash his face. She was still whimpering when he pulled on his pajama bottoms and left the bedroom.

In the kitchen, he put on a pot of coffee. While it was brewing, he turned on the news to see what they were saying today about the missing celebrity. It had taken until nightfall for anyone to finally figure out she was actually missing, or at least it had taken that long for it to make it into the news cycle, and today they were running with it. A large reward was being offered for information leading to her return.

Mark smiled to himself. No amount of money was worth the treasure he had locked in his closet. Muting the TV, he sat back to think. The scratches on his cheek were starting to sting. Things weren't going quite as smoothly as he had imagined they would the day before, when she had seemed a lot more compliant.

No matter. Mark liked a challenge. It was like developing a really intricate computer program. Sometimes you had to go back again and again, even to rethink the whole design. He would have to rethink a little here. Ms. Hunter was exhibiting that fiery will she displayed so effectively in *Lovers Quarrel*, one of his favorites. That was all very well, but eventually she would learn to control that spirit — to subvert it to his will.

Mark could still hear Alana crying out from time to time as he made and ate his breakfast. Not that anyone but he would hear her. The next property was a half mile away. Still, it was distracting, so he went into his study and closed the door. Soon he was lost in computer code, focused entirely on his work.

~*~

"Breathe," Alana ordered herself with the last vestige of her strength. Her throat hurt from screaming, and she was too exhausted to call out any longer. "Deep, cleansing breaths." *In…and out. In…and out.* She tried to expand her lungs and fill them with air, but it felt as if there were a two-ton weight on her chest, as if the darkness itself were crushing her.

After the nightmare of being abducted, bound, beaten and raped, being forced into the terrifying confines of this cage was the last push that threatened to send her flying into the abyss. She was alone in the pitch black, in the deafening silence. Panic threatened like an oncoming wave, but she knew if she gave in now, she would lose her mind.

"Calm yourself, manage the anxiety, challenge

the negative thinking, let the panic wash over you," she whispered, reminding herself of the techniques the phobia therapist had taught her. How had her abductor known of her fear of confined spaces? As far as she knew, it was one thing she'd managed to keep out of the media's endlessly voracious gossip machine.

"You can do this. You can do this," she promised herself. "Remember your anxiety map, and navigate through it."

This couldn't go on much longer. Her rescuers would be coming soon—they had to be. She was Alana Hunter—she would have been missed the instant she didn't show at the shoot. But how would they find her? Her phone was somewhere on the George Washington Bridge, crushed and destroyed.

Maybe the doorman had seen the car her abductor had used. Maybe street cameras had caught the license plate. Yes! They would track down the car, and it would lead them to the madman who held her prisoner. Already the police were probably closing in on the property, the SWAT team ready to burst in at any second.

Okay. Good. She was breathing again, the panic receding. She shifted in a vain attempt to get more comfortable. Her stomach, so long empty, had curled itself into a hard, painful knot, and her tongue felt like it was covered in sandpaper.

"But you're alive," she whispered aloud. "The guy is obviously insane, but if he'd been planning to kill you, wouldn't he have done it by now?"

Something brushed her face, and Alana screamed, jerking sharply in the tight confines of the small prison. Her heart was beating so hard she feared it would smash right out of her chest.

"A house spider, a harmless nothing little bug," she murmured as she willed herself to calm down once more. She focused on her breathing again, while trying to remember some of the affirmations the phobia coach had taught her.

Her thoughts drifted to the moment she'd entered the studio car. Her very first thought upon seeing the new driver was how much better looking he was than Hank. For a second she'd even wondered if he was an actor — someone sexy and new to the acting scene. He had thick golden-blond hair that hung over a high, smooth forehead, and intelligent green eyes. She had liked his long Roman nose and the generous mouth that was quirking into a nervous smile as she looked at him. She'd assumed his nerves were a result of meeting a famous actress in the flesh, but how wrong she'd been.

There was that horrible moment of realization that they were going the wrong way. When he'd pulled the gun, icy terror had shot through her body, leaving her dizzy and nauseated, her hands shaking. Her heart had pumped so hard she could feel it banging against her ribs and thumping in her ears. Yet here she was, still alive and relatively intact.

She was Alana Hunter, damn it, and this creep would never get away with what he'd done. She just needed to bide her time until the police arrived to rescue her. Meanwhile, she'd be damned if she was going to simply bow down and become this nut job's sex slave, or whatever the hell it was he wanted from her. The bastard had picked the wrong woman to abduct.

Brave words, but they rang hollow in her head. Who was she kidding? She was alone—all alone with a crazy man who seemed to both adore and despise her, who was intent on terrorizing her one moment, and comforting her the next. He had chained her, whipped her and raped her. Then he'd kissed away her tears, holding her tenderly in a warm, strong embrace, whispering sweet, soothing things, as if he hadn't been the one to torture her.

It would almost have been better if he'd just been a total brute, a pure monster. Who the hell was this guy and what in god's name did he want with her?

Hiding her face in her arms, Alana gave way to her tears.

~*~

About two hours later, Mark went to check on his charge. She was huddled in one corner of the cage, her arms wrapped protectively around herself. Her face was puffy and wet with tears, her eyes red from crying. Mark's heart went out to his darling girl. But he knew he had to be firm. She had to understand who was in charge.

"Alana."

She didn't respond. Mark went over to the cage and unlocked the small door. Reaching in, he dragged her forward, hauling her out of the cage. He pulled her upright and she stumbled, but Mark held her arm firmly, not allowing her to fall.

Without a word, he led her down the hall and through the bedroom into the bathroom. "Climb in the tub. Naughty girls don't get to use the toilet. You will pee in the tub."

Alana stared at him, her mouth opening, no doubt in another protest. Mark stopped her by placing two fingers against her lips. "No. You do not speak. Not a word. You climb in the tub and you spread your legs and pee like a good girl. If you protest or resist in any way, I'll put you back in the cage."

The threat worked. Alana got into the tub. Mark turned on the warm water, and as it splashed against the porcelain, a stream of urine cascaded between her shapely legs, while she blushed sweetly, her face averted.

When she was done, he allowed her to wash off, and dry herself with a towel. She kept her mouth shut for a change, which pleased him. Maybe he was finally getting through to her.

Taking her back into the bedroom, he had her sit on the bed while he went to the closet. Choosing a soft jersey of dark pink cotton, Mark returned to his slave girl. "I like dresses on a woman. You won't be wearing pants anymore, and of course no bra or underwear. I bought you a whole wardrobe, my darling. When you have learned to behave better, you might earn the right to some of the finer ones. But for now this will do. Lift your arms."

She obeyed, and he slid the dress over her head. It fit her perfectly, but then, she would look good in a potato sack. Reaching into the nightstand, he withdrew a short silver chain, which he attached between the slave bracelets on her wrists. "You tried to escape from me earlier, and you tried to cause me harm. You obviously can't yet be trusted," he explained. "So for now you will be treated as a prisoner."

He half expected her to protest, but she remained silent. "I know you must be hungry, little girl," he said. "Perhaps hunger will sharpen your desire to be obedient." She pressed her lips together, and he could see her swallow. Yes, she was hungry.

Mark led her down the hall to the living room, where he settled on the couch. Alana stood in front of him, staring at the floor. He pressed her shoulders, forcing her to her knees. "You will kneel on the floor for your first lesson in how to address your Master."

He lifted her chin, forcing her to look at him. "First rule, you will always respond to me when I speak to you. You will answer promptly and with proper respect. You will reply to commands with 'Yes, Sir,' or 'Yes, Mark'. You will answer any and all direct questions. Other than that, you will not speak unless spoken to. If there is something you must say, you will ask first for permission to speak. Is that clearly understood?"

He dropped her chin and again she looked down. No response. Mark felt anger rising but he forced it down. He narrowed his eyes and set his mouth in a grim smile. "All right then. Since you insist, we will go about this a different way."

He stood and pulled Alana to her feet. Dragging her to the wall by the fireplace, he took down a large reproduction of a painting by Marc Chagall. He had read once in an interview that Alana especially liked Chagall's work.

Her back against the wall, he raised her manacled wrists above her head and hung the chain over the hook. His heart gave a tug, along with his cock. She looked so pretty and defenseless, her luxuriant hair in a tumble around her face, her nipples poking through the thin fabric of her dress.

"Alana?"

Silence.

Then the sharp crack of his palm against her soft cheek.

Alana cried out.

"Alana?"

Nothing but her heavy breathing. A red mark appeared on her face where his palm had struck her. Again he slapped her, this time across the other cheek. Again and again he said her name, waiting for her reply, slapping her each time she failed to respond, until her face was bright red from the blows, her cheeks wet with tears. Yet still the stubborn girl remained silent.

Furious, Mark gave up. Lifting her dress high, he tucked it around her neck and shoulders. She looked ridiculous with her dress hiked up, her body naked but for the curled dark hair that covered her delicate mons.

Roughly, he grabbed her by the pubic hair, using it to pull her away from the wall. He fingered her cunt for several minutes, forcing her pussy to secrete its juices, despite her best efforts to resist him.

Slapping her thighs, he forced her legs farther apart. Again his strong fingers found her cunt and he slid two at once deep into her defenseless body. He felt the heat of those velvet walls and longed to thrust his rock-hard cock into her. But she didn't deserve his cock. Not now. Not yet.

Mark continued to forcibly arouse his chained slave until she was moaning despite herself. Alana's face was averted and her eyes were squeezed shut, but Mark knew from her wet pussy and her ragged breathing that he was getting to her. When her body began to move, her hips arching slightly toward his hand, he pulled away, calculatedly leaving the bound woman unsatisfied. She wouldn't be coming for a while. She would have to earn her way into his good graces.

"Alana, listen to me," he said quietly, standing back to admire her heaving breasts, the nipples suffused with blood so that they looked like ripe cherries. He held his fingers to his nose and inhaled her spicy-sweet fragrance. "You will stay on that wall. You will keep your chain on that hook, and you will keep your dress up on your shoulders. I'm going to work for a while. When I come back, if your arms are down, or your dress has fallen, you will be punished severely. If you try anything stupid like trying to get away, I'll kill you. It's that simple."

Alana opened her eyes wide, fixing him with a terrified look, but still the wretched girl said nothing.

Turning on his heel, Mark left her alone, naked and chained to the wall.

She would learn what it was to suffer. He would see to that.

Mark returned to the living room an hour later, a bottle of water in his hand. Alana's head was turned to the side, resting against her shoulder, her eyes closed. She didn't seem to hear him come in. He was pleased to see her wrists were still slung over the picture hook, her dress still bunched around her shoulders. Perhaps progress was finally being made.

He set down the bottle on the end table by the couch and approached her. "Alana?" he said softly. He held his breath as he waited.

Slowly, she lifted her head and opened her eyes. "Yes, Sir," she finally answered in a hoarse whisper.

Mark smiled broadly. "Good girl." Gently, he lifted her bound wrists up and over the hook. Her arms fell heavily in front of her. They were icy to the touch. Smoothing down her dress, Mark scooped her into his arms and carried her to the couch. Settling with her in his lap, he took her lifeless arms between his large, strong hands and gently massaged the life back into her limbs.

"Thirsty," she whispered huskily.

Mark carefully set her limp body on the couch and sat beside her, reaching for the bottle of water. He held it to her lips and she drank, hesitantly at first, then greedily. It was mid-afternoon and she had had nothing to eat or drink since the champagne the evening before, and, now that he thought about it, she'd barely eaten a thing since he'd picked her up.

He allowed her to finish the bottle. Standing, he pulled off his T-shirt. He preened a moment in front of her, proud of his muscular physique, but Alana didn't appear to notice. With a shrug, he sat beside her and unlocked the chain between her wrists so he could slip off her dress. Once she was stripped naked, he cradled her again in his arms, holding her body close to his.

He kissed the top of her head. "Are you ready to try again, slave girl?"

"Yes, Sir," she said in a low, uninflected voice.

Mark was elated. "Good, darling. Here's the first thing. I guess it's because of your career and all — a famous actress used to having her way in everything — but you are too proud. That's what I think. And pride no longer has a place in your life. Do you understand that?"

Alana didn't respond.

Mark pushed down the sudden annoyance. It was one step forward, three steps back with this girl. But she looked so woebegone, so exhausted, that he took pity on her.

"You're tired, so I'll forgive you that lapse, but remember—speak when spoken to. Answer my direct questions." He patted her head, brightening as he added, "You obviously need another spanking. I want you to lie over my knee like the naughty little girl you are. I'm going to remind you to behave."

Mark's cock ached as he forced the girl down over his lap. He twisted so he could insert his knee between her thighs in order to force her legs apart. With one hand, he massaged and caressed her gorgeous ass. As she wriggled, he used his other hand to stroke and tease her cunt. Keeping one hand on her sex, he began to swat her ass.

He worked her up more quickly this time, and it wasn't long before her ass turned bright red, the skin hot to the touch. Alana was wailing and whimpering as she struggled on his lap. "Please, please stop," she begged.

"If I stop, will you behave?"

"Yes! Please!"

"Please what?"

"Please stop spanking me! I can't take this. It hurts! It hurts!" Her last word ended in a high-pitched wail.

Satisfied, Mark lowered his arm. He had her just where he wanted her. Alana's body sagged with relief against him. His fingers were still buried in her pussy, and he kept her pinned beneath his thigh.

"Okay, then. I'm going to take you on your word that you'll behave. The first thing you must learn is how to address me properly. How to respond when spoken to." He paused to make sure she was paying attention

"First of all, what are you, Alana?"

"I—I don't know what you mean," she sniffled.

He lifted her from his lap and set her on her bottom beside him. She winced as her tender ass made contact with the cushions. She wrapped her arms protectively around her torso. He allowed her that cover, for the moment.

"I'll tell you what you are, so you will know." He paused a beat, then said, "You are my slave. You are my slut. You are my whore. You are my cunt. When I ask you what you are, you may answer with any one of those terms."

Alana lay still, but made no protest. Perhaps she was just too tired and defeated after the last thirty-six hours of confusion and torture. Or perhaps she was finally accepting her lot.

"So, tell me, Alana. What are you?"

"Your slave."

"Your slave, *Sir*," he emphasized.

"Your slave, Sir," she repeated woodenly.

"What else?"

"Um, your slut, uh, Sir." She looked away.

"Look at me when I speak to you," he insisted, and slowly she turned her head to face him. "So you admit you are my slave and my slut. What else are you?"

"I—I can't remember."

"You are my whore. My cunt. Repeat it."

"I, um, I'm your whore, Sir." She said it without conviction.

"And?"

"I'm, I…" she trailed off, whispering something incomprehensible.

"Say it! What are you? Say it, or you'll get a whipping and then you'll say it."

Alana winced but answered in a barely audible voice. "I'm your cunt, Sir." She blushed deeply, the color mottling her cheeks and neck.

Mark was touched by her innocence. "That's right. You're my cunt. Why does that make you blush? I can see we will have to desensitize you to that particular word. That will be your pet name for now. You are my cunt. And you also have a lovely cunt. Later, I'll have you display your lovely cunt to me, but for now you can stay on my lap. Your nickname is now cunt girl, until I decide to change it. Understand, cunt girl?"

Throughout his speech the color in her face and neck continued to rise. Mark was delighted with her sensitivity. She was adorable. "And now, cunt girl," he went on sadistically, "I'll teach you more about what and who you are. Do you know why you exist?"

Alana looked confused and Mark went on. "You exist to serve me. Now, I'll ask you again. Why do you exist, cunt girl?"

"To," she hesitated, but forced the words to her lips. " — to serve you, Sir."

"That's correct. You exist to serve me, but you don't yet deserve me." He flashed a grin, pleased with his turn of phrase. "Not yet. What you deserve is to be beaten for your bratty, willful behavior." He gave her a moment to absorb this. Then, with a school teacher's patience, he asked, "Now, what do you deserve?"

"To be beaten." Her voice caught in her throat.

"To be beaten what?"

"To be beaten, Sir."

"Good. And not only do you deserve to be beaten, you deserve to be punished for your sins. Now. What do you deserve?"

"I deserve to be beaten, Sir," she replied tremulously. "And to be punished for my sins."

"That's right," Mark said, nodding approvingly. "And the way you are to be punished is up to me. Whatever I decree is what you deserve. Understand, cunt girl?"

"Yes, Sir." Her eyes were round with fear.

His cock was swelling in his jeans, but he continued with the lesson. "Now, cunt, I am your Master. You must be willing to suffer for me. Who am I?"

"My Master, Sir."

"And what are you willing to do for me, slave?"

"To suffer for you, Sir."

"Yes. To suffer for me, with grace. I'll teach you grace, cunt girl. And I will teach you what it is to suffer."

Alana didn't respond.

"Now, let's start again."

Over and over Mark drilled Alana in how he expected her to respond. After another thirty minutes or so of questions and answers he was satisfied.

"All right then, cunt girl, time to go back to the cage. I'm going to eat some lunch but I don't expect you are hungry."

"Please, Sir, I'm *so* hungry. Please, I did everything you said."

"No. You aren't hungry, cunt girl. Your Master says you aren't hungry."

She whimpered but said nothing.

"Now, are you hungry, cunt?" Mark prodded.

"No, Sir," Alana whispered faintly, tears welling in her eyes and spilling down her cheeks.

"No, I didn't think so." He fingered the

scratches Alana had made on his face that morning.
She seemed to understand his silent rebuke. He
stood up, lifting the girl in his arms and gently
setting her on her feet. He gestured for her to kneel
on the ground next to the couch.

"Since you have yet to prove that you are more
than an animal — an animal that scratches and
bites — I'm going to treat you like an animal for a
while longer. Wait there by the couch and don't
move."

She knelt obediently, fear etched onto her pretty
face.

Mark went over to a large chest in the corner of
the room. Whips, riding crops, collars, leashes and
various other toys were stowed inside. Mark pulled
out a heavy collar of black iron with a single ring
hanging in the front. He also removed a long leash
made of thick metal links. Returning to Alana, he
set the implements down next to her.

"Lift your hair," he instructed her. Alana lifted
her heavy mane of dark hair, baring her long,
slender neck, and the graceful gesture took his
breath away.

He attached the heavy collar around her neck.
He liked the way it hung on her chest, the ring
sitting just above the rounded swell of her breasts.

"This is your animal collar, cunt girl. I'll remove it when you stop acting like an animal. Till then it remains. Here is your leash." He attached it to the ring on the center of the collar and jerked her upward. "Get on your feet."

Once she was upright, he led her by the leash back into the bedroom and toward the closet. "You're going back in the cage."

"Oh, please," she begged, pulling back. "Not the cage. Please, Sir. Please, I'm begging you."

"Disobedient animals belong in cages, Alana." He jerked her forward. "Are you refusing your Master's direct command?" Mark lifted his eyebrows, daring her to defy him.

Alana bit her lower lip. Finally, she whispered, "No, Sir."

"All right then." He removed the leash and forced her to her knees. Pointing to the open door of the cage, he ordered, "Crawl in. If you take your punishment with submissive grace, I might let you eat something later. Meanwhile, get some rest if you can. I have lots of fun things planned."

After she crawled into the small space and curled up on its floor, Mark padlocked the door and left the closet, closing the doors behind him.

Chapter 4

Hungry. Thirsty. So thirsty. Throat hurts, eyes sting. Every muscle aches. Exhausted. What was I thinking, trying to fight him? He's much bigger, much stronger. He has a gun. He holds all the cards. I was stupid to resist. I need to pretend. I'm an actress. I can act. I can behave as if I'm buying into his total insanity. I can submit.

Alana opened her eyes wide, trying to see something in the dark closet. She focused on the line of light showing beneath the doors. Was he out there, waiting? Would he let her out soon? Should she call out, pretend to be contrite, apologize and promise to be a good girl?

She opened her mouth, but no sound would come. She couldn't do it. She wouldn't beg. He could fuck himself.

Mark lay on the bed. Alana had looked so miserable and terrified as he'd forced her back into the cage. He scanned his memory for any discussion in the many blogs and fan sites of her having a fear of small spaces, but there had been no mention—he would have remembered.

It was just another sign that they were made for each other—he had honed in on her secret fear, and wasn't afraid to capitalize on it—for her own good, of course. She had to be punished for her misbehavior or she would never learn. She needed to understand that his word was law.

She had stopped her whimpering. Maybe she had fallen asleep, the poor dear—she had to be exhausted. Mark closed his eyes and drifted in and out of a doze. When he awoke, the sun was already setting outside the window. He must have been worn out from all the excitement of the past few days.

There was still no sound from the closet. He would let her out soon. Getting to his feet, he went into the kitchen to make his girl something substantial to eat. He couldn't have her passing out on him because of no food, nor did he want to starve her to death.

He cooked a steak and fried some potatoes, the delicious smells awakening his appetite. Leaving the food on the stove, he returned to the bedroom closet and pulled open the doors. Flicking on the light, he peered down at the girl curled in the small space, her hair obscuring her face.

As he crouched down in front of the cage, she moaned and lifted her head. "Please," she croaked. "Please let me out."

Tenderness surged through Mark's heart. She looked so pathetic, her large eyes pleading. She'd been punished enough, for now. He quickly unlocked the padlock and opened the small door. He helped her as she maneuvered her way out of the confines of the metal cage and rose unsteadily to her feet.

He took the leash from the hook where he'd left it and attached it to her collar. "Are you ready to behave, sweetheart?"

"Yes, Sir," she replied obediently.

A thrill shot through him. "Good girl. I've made you some food."

He led her to the kitchen, moving slowly so she could keep up without stumbling. When she attempted to take a seat at the table, he pulled her leash gently downward. "Have you forgotten? Slave girls don't sit on furniture. You kneel at your

Master's feet."

She didn't protest, but sank to the cushion he'd thoughtfully placed on the floor beside his chair.

He wrapped the end of the leash around the back of his chair. "Put your hands behind your back," he instructed as he took the wrist chain from his pocket. Moving behind her, he clipped her bracelets together.

"Please," she said in a tremulous voice. "I'm so hungry. How can I eat if my wrists are cuffed?"

"I'm going to feed you, cunt girl," he replied, amused at her wince, which he assumed was because of her new pet name.

He slid the steak and mound of fried potatoes onto a plate and brought it to the table. Returning to the counter, he took out a glass and filled it with water from the tap. Taking his seat at the table, he cut a small piece of the meat and held it to her lips.

Alana opened her mouth like a baby bird and eagerly accepted the morsel. Chewing quickly, she opened her mouth again.

Mark didn't speak as he fed his slave girl. He felt at once powerful and benevolent. He literally held this creature's life in his hands. For a moment, Mark stopped feeding her as he marveled anew at her beauty. Her hair was a tangled mess around her face, but that just added to her wanton, wild look. With the heavy collar above her bare, beautiful breasts, she was like a barely tamed animal.

And she belonged to him!

With great self-control, he resisted the impulse to throw her down and fuck her right there on the kitchen floor. There would be time, plenty of time, he reminded himself.

He ate the food along with her, alternating bites between them, and sharing the water. When they'd finished the food, he brought over a small wine glass and a bottle of his favorite port. He poured a generous serving into the glass and inhaled its sweet aroma.

He took a sip and then held it to Alana's lips. "This is an excellent port. Have some."

Alana sipped. Mark took another swallow. He let her sip some more. "I'm very pleased with you, cunt girl. You've made a lot of progress in just one day. You have the potential to become a worthy slave. I know you aren't here of your own free will. I'm not stupid enough to think you're obeying at this point for any reason other than you have no choice in the matter. Still, you are behaving well, even as a prisoner."

She said nothing to this, and he quashed his slight irritation that she hadn't responded positively to his praise.

Getting to his feet, he unwound the leash from the chair and gave it a tug. "Stand up," he commanded tersely. "I want to see your body."

Alana got somewhat awkwardly to her feet, her hands still secured behind her back.

Mark assessed her dispassionately. Her pubic hair had surprised him. He'd gotten used to shaved women, which were the norm on all the porn sites he frequented. He almost wanted to keep Alana's sparse curls for the sheer novelty, but of course a slave had to be fully accessible to her Master. Beyond the physical aspect of baring oneself, there was a mental aspect as well—the vulnerability created by being completely exposed and open to him.

He was feeling expansive, and decided to make the experience a relatively pleasant one for her. "I'm going to give you a bath," he informed her.

In the bathroom, he allowed her to use the toilet as he drew the bath water in the freestanding, claw-footed tub that had come with the old place, and which he'd left when refinishing the bathroom, because it was just like the one in *Lovers' Quarrel*. Would she notice?

Mark stripped off his jeans and shirt so they wouldn't get wet, though he kept on his underwear. He flicked on the wall heater, and got out the fancy bath oil and the pretty pink razor he'd purchased just for her, along with a small pair of barber's scissors. He set the items on the floor beside the tub and poured several capfuls of oil into the steaming water. As the water rose in the bath, he removed the heavy chain collar from around Alana's neck and unlocked her wrists.

He gestured toward the steaming water. "Climb in."

She did as she was told, gingerly lowering herself into the hot, scented water.

Mark crouched beside the tub. Directing her to lean her head back, he washed her long, dark hair, shampooing the silky tresses and rinsing them with a small plastic pitcher. Alana was as passive as a baby as he ministered to her. When he was done, he twisted a towel around her head.

Next, using a large soft washcloth, he started with her breasts, rubbing the soapy cloth over her nipples, pleased as they rose to his touch.

Alana rested her head against the lip of the tub and closed her eyes. She seemed to be relaxing at last. The tension that had held her body rigid seemed to be draining from her. Perhaps she just didn't have the energy, the strength of will to resist him any longer. Or perhaps, just perhaps, she was coming to trust him the slightest bit.

Mark moved the cloth over her smooth, firm stomach, and on down to the pubic hair he planned to remove. He rubbed the curls until they were frothy with soap. "Spread your legs," he ordered. When Alana didn't instantly comply he said, "Do I have to hold you under the water to make you obey?"

That got a quick response, and Alana opened her long, slender legs wide.

Mark soaped her inner thighs, his already erect cock hardening to steel as he moved the cloth slowly but inexorably toward her spread pussy.

Alana sat up a little straighter in the tub, her body tensing as she brought her legs together.

"Hey, what do you think you're doing?" Mark slapped at her knees. "Don't you dare close yourself to me. Unless you want to find out just how long you can hold your breath."

She let her knees fall open once more, and Mark set the washcloth aside. Using his fingers, he gently stroked her cunt beneath the oily water, finding her clit and rubbing it lightly.

Alana actually sighed as her head fell back once again, her eyes fluttering shut. Excited, Mark placed his other hand on a breast, which was just peeking above the water. He kept his other hand between her legs and pressed a finger inside her.

As he teased and stroked her cunt, Alana moaned, a shudder of pleasure moving through her frame.

Yes.

He played with her a while longer, until he was nearly on the edge of coming himself. Recalling himself to his task, Mark took his hands from the water and reached for the razor. "I'm going to shave you," he informed the girl, who had remained still, her eyes closed.

She opened her eyes, the alarm clear on her face.

"Relax," Mark said with a laugh. "I'll start with your legs. Then the underarms, and finally your pretty little cunt." He touched the scratches on his cheeks as he added, "Don't worry, I won't cut you." He reached for the bottle of oil and added briskly, "Lift your left leg over the side of the tub so I have access."

"Please," she said. "I can do that."

"Of course you can," he agreed. "But you're not going to. I am. You are my possession to do with as I please. The sooner you understand that, the easier things will go for you. Now, do as you're told."

With obvious reluctance, Alana lifted her gorgeous leg and rested it along the side of the tub. Mark squirted some oil on her skin and denuded it in smooth, even strokes. Moving around the tub, he did the second leg. "There, see? I know what I'm doing," he said, pleased with himself. "Lift your left arm."

She didn't protest, though he could see she wanted to. Progress.

When he'd carefully shaved her smooth, he turned his focus at last to her pussy. "We could do wax," he mused as he regarded her. "But I do like the idea of a blade against your cunt." He smiled at her gasp. A sudden, glittering image of her chained against a wall as he held a long, sharp blade to her smooth cunt and pressed the tip against her skin leaped into his mind's eye.

"Please," she entreated, snapping him from his

reverie. "You're scaring me."

He lifted his lips into a cruel, amused smile. "Good. A little fear is a good thing, Alana. It reminds you of your place." He let the water drain from the tub until it was low enough to leave her body accessible to him.

First, he trimmed her pubes as closely as possible to the skin. She held herself very still during the process—a wise move. He let the rest of the water out of the tub. Though the room was warm from the steam and the heater, the naked girl shivered, goosebumps rising on her flesh.

Mark squirted some of the oil directly on what was left of Alana's pubic hair. He picked up the razor and leaned over the tub to get a good angle. He began to shave her, moving the razor carefully over her mons until she was smooth.

Alana watched with wide eyes all the while.

"Lift your hips and spread your legs so I can get at your labia," he instructed. "And don't move. I don't want to nick you."

She obeyed, her body trembling, though whether from cold or fear, he wasn't certain. With slow, careful strokes, Mark shaved the delicate skin until it was as soft as satin. Satisfied, he ran the bath water again, filling the tub with warm water to rinse her.

When he finally had her climb out, she reached for the towel he held in his hands, but he shook his head. "No. I'm ministering to you right now. I will dry you."

She stood and shifted obediently as he directed while he toweled her dry. He removed the towel from her head and carefully brushed her wet, tangled hair smooth before tucking the damp locks behind her ears.

Satisfied, he spread a fresh towel on the counter beside the sink. "Get up here and spread your legs. I want to taste you."

She looked confused for a moment. Then, apparently understanding, she blushed dark red.

"Go on," he urged. "I'm going to lick that pretty, smooth cunt, and if you're a very good girl, I might even let you come." He hoisted her up onto the towel and forced her thighs wide. Crouching in front of her, he admired her cunt, which really was a work of art, like an orchid in bloom, the petals dark pink fading to purple.

Bringing his face close, he inhaled the sweet aroma of bath oil and feminine musk. Placing his hands on her thighs to keep them apart, he licked lightly along the smooth, satiny soft folds of her pussy. As he licked in circles around her clit, Alana moaned, ever so softly.

Excited, he let his tongue flick directly over the hood of her clit. Taking his time, he licked and suckled her until she was moaning in earnest, her breath coming fast. "Oh," she sighed. "Oh, oh, oh…" She was trembling, her chest heaving, clearly on the edge of a powerful orgasm.

Abruptly, Mark pulled away from her. "Alana," he said, his own lust barely controlled, "I know you're about to come, but slave girls have to pay for their orgasms. Are you willing to pay?"

She frowned, fear in her eyes. "I—I don't know. I'm afraid you're going to hurt me again." Her voice trembled.

"I will hurt you, yes," he agreed pleasantly, though his cock was about to burst with excitement. "Pain is good for the submissive soul. You'll appreciate the pleasure that much more keenly. I'm going to teach you to associate pain and pleasure. To endure the one to achieve the other. I'm going to teach you that to suffer can be sublime."

No longer panting with lust, she tried to close

her legs, but he wouldn't let her, his hands still firmly on her thighs. "I don't want to learn that," she dared.

"No one asked you what you wanted," he informed her. "It's about what you need. And you need to suffer." He reached for the hairbrush with one hand, the other still on her thigh. "Let's see," he pretended to muse, though he knew exactly what he was going to do. "Since it's your cunt that is so needy, your cunt will take the pain."

Her eyes on the brush, Alana again tried to shut her legs.

Mark removed his hand but directed sharply, "Keep your legs open, if you know what's good for you. Wide open. If you try to close them again, I'll tie you down." Making his tone gentler, he continued, "You want the pleasure. You must learn to take the pain that goes with it."

Fear etched on her face, Alana spread her legs again. She looked ravishing, her eyes wide, her cheeks flushed, her nipples dark against the cream of her flesh.

Mark adjusted his painfully erect cock in his underwear and took a step back. "I'm going to beat your pussy with the hairbrush, Alana. Because you're so new, I'll only give you ten strokes this time. But if you close your legs or resist in any way, you'll forfeit the right to come. Understand?"

Alana swallowed visibly but finally nodded, her violet eyes wide with fear.

"I didn't hear you."

"Yes, Sir," she said in a tremulous voice.

Holding the handle, he lightly smacked her denuded cunt first with the bristles to sensitize the delicate skin. Predictably, she yelped with each strike. At the count of five, he turned it over and struck her with the unforgiving wood. The smack resounded against the tiled walls, followed by Alana's plaintive cry. To her credit, she managed to maintain her position, legs spread wide, hands clenched into fists on either side of her body.

Mark was counting to himself, and he brought the tenth stroke down much harder than the preceding nine. As he expected, Alana screamed and slammed her legs shut. She didn't yet have the discipline to resist her own impulses. That would come with time.

"Oh, dear," he said with mock sympathy. "You closed your legs, you naughty girl. No orgasm for you."

She was whimpering steadily and rocking

slightly forward and back, her arms now wrapped around her torso. Zero discipline. He had a lot of work to do. But first, he needed to fuck her.

He pulled down his underwear and kicked it away. Grabbing the oil bottle, he squirted some onto his fingers and coated his cock with it. Reaching for her waist, he pulled her forward onto his cock, entering her with one hard, perfect thrust. She wailed, fear and pain in the sound, but this only spurred him on. She might be in hell at the moment, but he — he was definitely in heaven.

Chapter 5

How had the week flown by so fast? In the six days he'd held her captive, Alana was progressing well, at least in terms of her behavior. She obeyed his dictates, for the most part, though she did have to be reminded from time to time, either with words, or with his whip.

He no longer had her wear the heavy chain collar, except occasionally during a session in the dungeon. He found it got in the way when he wanted to fuck her—it was too clunky. Instead, he placed a leather dog collar around her neck from time to time, to remind her of her status. Someday, when she earned it, he'd buy her a true slave collar—one she wore not because she had to, but because she wanted to.

She had stopped begging him to let her go, and had given up on the idea that she would soon be rescued. She barely spoke at all, except in answer to a direct question. This was okay, if a little lonely at times. For now, it was enough just to have her near him. When she was better trained, he would allow her to speak more freely.

Though he longed to have her of her own free will, he'd come to understand that process might take longer than he'd expected. The thought that it might never happen was unendurable, so he put it from his mind.

Still, what they shared was better, far better, than nothing. Alana Hunter, long adored from afar, was here, in his home, in his arms, whenever he wanted her. She belonged to him, if not in spirit, at least in body. For now, that was enough.

She remained a hot topic on the news, of course, with wild speculation about all sorts of possibilities, from a routine kidnapping with a requested and exorbitant ransom only a matter of time, to her having run off with a secret billionaire prince from somewhere in the Middle East. Popular opinion on the many social media forums was beginning to edge toward her being dead, which was what Mark hoped the authorities would also come to conclude.

He was careful never to let her out of the house. On the occasions when he had to leave her to run errands or check his mailbox at the post office in the nearby village, he always chained her on the bed by both wrists and ankles. He gagged her, too, on the very unlikely chance anyone might stop by. No one knew where he lived except the utility companies and the UPS guy, and he intended to keep it that way.

Though the police held press conferences and pretended they were following leads, so far there had been nothing to connect him to her disappearance. Even though there was some grainy camera footage of the car he'd bought for the sole purpose of her abduction, the stolen plates had, as he'd hoped, completely thrown them off the track. His real car, the one registered in his real name, was in the driveway. The sedan he'd purchased for the abduction was safely tucked away in the old barn behind his house, and there it would remain for the foreseeable future.

He made sure Alana didn't hear any news at all. He didn't want to upset her. Perhaps someday he would allow her to contact her family, but only when the two of them came to a very different understanding. For now, he was all the family she needed.

He allowed her to sleep next to him at night, though still chained, of course. He kept her tethered to the ringbolt in the wall when in his bed, but with enough slack in the restraints for her to sleep comfortably. Sometimes he would fuck her just before falling asleep, and drift off with his cock still buried inside of her.

Often, he would awaken in the night and it would take a moment to realize she was really there beside him. After years of dreaming of her, living vicariously through her films, it was still hard to believe she was there in the flesh.

If he awoke with an erection, which he usually did, he would take her then and there. Sometimes he liked to rouse her by straddling her chest and forcing his hard cock into her mouth. She would wake up spluttering and choking, but he would hold her still, forcing her to take his cock and make him come. He wouldn't withdraw until he had shot his load deep into her throat.

Other times he would flip her over and fuck her like a dog, not even caring if she woke up or not. Of course, she always did wake up. Sometimes she would cry out in pain if he entered her too quickly. "That's your fault, Alana," he would tell her. "If you were a proper slave, you would always be wet and ready whenever I wanted you."

One night, the moon woke him some time after midnight. It had risen high, filling the room with silvery light. Mark lifted himself on his elbow to admire his sleeping prize. As if feeling his gaze upon her, she opened her eyes.

"I need to fuck you," he announced, his erection instant at the mere thought. Then another idea entered his head as he looked at his naked, beautiful slave girl. He reached for the lamp beside the bed, since he'd need more light than the moon could provide for what he had in mind.

Turning back to Alana, he said, "Come for me, slave. I want to watch you masturbate."

She looked startled, a pretty pink flush moving over her cheeks. "What?"

"You heard me. Make yourself come. Use your hand. I want to watch. And don't forget to ask for permission to orgasm."

When she didn't immediately obey, he slapped her across the face. "Do what the fuck I tell you, slave," he said in a hard voice. "Don't make me ask again."

Tears welled in her eyes, her hand flying to her cheek. But after a moment, she spread her legs dutifully. Licking her fingers, she dropped her slender hand between them.

Mark shifted so he could see her cunt better. As she began to touch herself, her eyes fluttered shut.

"No," Mark said. "Keep your eyes open and focused on your Master. And do it like you mean it. I want a good show. If I'm not pleased, I'll put you in the cage."

That got her attention. She really hated that cage. She stroked herself, her eyes locked on his. After a while, she began to breathe faster, her chest rising and falling as she frigged herself in rapid, swirling strokes.

Mark fisted his cock and massaged himself as he watched his beautiful slave bring herself to the brink of orgasm.

"Oh," she breathed, her body suddenly tensing. She continued to rub herself, her eyes going unfocused, her mouth slackening. All at once, she shuddered in a series of small spasms, her fingers flying over her swollen cunt.

Watching her come made him come, too, and Mark aimed his shooting ejaculate over her breasts, catching both erect nipples with his flow. Her eyes were closed, her hair wild on the pillow, a pink orgasmic flush over her chest and throat. Jesus Christ, she was so fucking hot.

Then, all at once, he realized what she'd forgotten. She would have to pay, the very naughty, naughty girl. He smiled cruelly as he regarded her, though he spoke with feigned gentleness.

"Oh dear," he said softly. "What did my slave girl forget to do?"

Her eyes flew open. "Sir?" she whispered, the fear ripe in her voice as she focused on his face.

"Think, cunt. What did I tell you to do before you came? What must you always do before coming?"

"Oh, gosh, I'm sorry. I for—" she began.

He cut her off. "Do you know what happens to a slut who comes without permission?"

No answer.

He grabbed her by the throat, just hard enough to get her attention. "I asked you a question." He squeezed harder, his thumb and index finger pressing into the soft flesh just below her jaw.

"N-no, Sir," she wheezed, barely able to form the words.

He continued to hold her by the throat, gripping it hard so that her face reddened, her eyes bugging out as she clawed ineffectually at his hands.

"She's punished," he told her, as if she didn't

know. "Soundly."

When he let her go, she gasped, sucking in air like a fish out of water. "Oh, please," she begged. "I'm sorry. Please don't punish me, Sir. I'll do — "

Again he cut her off. "You can't seem to keep your mouth shut tonight, can you? I'll have to help you then." He sat up and swung his legs over the side of the bed. Pulling open the nightstand drawer, he took out her ball gag. Getting to his feet, he pointed to the floor. "On your knees, cunt."

Alana scrambled from the bed and knelt in front of him. She knew better than to wipe his precious seed from her breasts. "Open wide," he said, bringing the rubber ball to her lips. He shoved it in and secured the harness tightly around her head.

Taking her arm, he hoisted her to her feet and led her down the hall to the dungeon playroom. The full moon cast the room in an eerie silver glow, and he quite liked the effect. He decided to leave off the lights as he led her to the pulley apparatus. Securing her arms above her on the suspension bar, he ratcheted up the bar until she was on tiptoe.

"Tonight we will use the cane."

Alana's eyes widened in terror. She was right to be afraid. The cane, if not used properly, could cut the flesh and permanently damage the skin. Luckily for her, Mark knew what he was doing. He would mark her flesh with lovely welts. They would remain for a day or two, a proper reminder of her failure to ask her Master for permission in all things.

Anticipatory tears rolled down her pretty face. Behind the bright red ball she made muffled, pleading sounds, but Mark was impervious.

"A slut who doesn't remember to ask permission must be punished. Do I make myself clear, cunt girl?"

Alana nodded miserably. She looked stunningly beautiful, her pale, supple flesh bathed in the silver of the moonlit night. Mark came very close to her and leaned down to kiss the top of her head. Bending lower, he kissed and lightly bit each beautiful nipple, tasting his own salty jism, which had dried there. Despite his recent climax, his cock began to harden again.

"Prepare," he said, as he walked slowly around the naked, suspended woman, "to suffer."

He brought the cane with a well-aimed thwack across her gorgeous ass.

Predictably, Alana screamed behind her gag and

swayed forward.

"Stay still," he barked. "Don't move out of position again. Take what's coming to you." He struck her again, adding another sexy welt just below the first. He loved the whistle of the rattan just before it made contact with flesh, then the deeply satisfying sound of impact, followed by her muffled, gurgling cry.

He let a sharp blow land against the backs of her thighs, and she twisted in her restraints. Because she was on tiptoe, she couldn't maintain her balance and swung around toward him. His cane, already in midflight for the next stroke, missed its intended target, instead striking her belly, the tip landing on her bare mons. At once, an angry red welt rose on the spot.

"Stupid girl," he said. "That was your fault."

Alana swayed in her chains, her eyes rolling upward. Alarmed, Mark dropped the cane. She was still conscious, though clearly on the verge of collapse. Quickly, Mark released her arms, catching her as she slumped down to the ground.

Though his initial impulse was to carry her to bed and cover her welts with kisses, she would never learn if she didn't fully experience the consequence of her actions. Rather than reward her for coming without permission and moving out of position, he had to complete the punishment.

Lifting her into his strong arms, he carried her into the bedroom and on into the closet. The cage door was ajar, and he maneuvered her into the small space. He unbuckled her gag and pulled it from her mouth. Then he shut the cage door and clicked the padlock into place.

Mark woke again as the sun was coming up. He'd left the closet doors open, and he listened a moment but heard no sound. Throwing back the covers, he got to his feet and went to check on his charge.

She was curled in her usual fetal ball, her back to him, her hair obscuring her face. Her ass was nicely welted with a series of red lines already fading to pink. As he came farther into the closet, she lifted her head slowly and twisted back to fix him with a pleading gaze.

Mark crouched down and unlocked the door, pulling it open. He helped her crawl from the cage and hoisted her to her feet. The welt across her sex was red and oozing slightly. Lifting her into his arms, Mark carried her to the bathroom.

He set her gently onto the toilet. While she was peeing, he ran a warm bath for her, adding a generous squirt of bath oil. She rose unsteadily to her feet and flushed the toilet. He moved quickly to her side and placed his arm around her shoulder. "You'll have a nice bath and I'll cleanse the wound," he said.

He helped Alana step into the tub. She winced as her tender, welted skin made contact with the water. As gently as if he were washing a child, Mark carefully soaped the wounded area. The spot where the tip had made contact was the worst. He hoped it wouldn't permanently scar her.

He thought about apologizing, but reminded himself she was to blame. If she ended up with a scar, it would be a silent reminder to exert better self-control.

He let her soak while he brushed his teeth, put on a pair of pajama bottoms and went to put on coffee. In case she got any stupid ideas, he locked the bathroom door from the outside, pleased he'd thought of everything when he'd remodeled the old farmhouse.

When he returned, he helped her from the tub and gently dried her off. The wound caused by the tip of the cane didn't look as bad now. He applied some triple antibiotic cream and covered it with some gauze and medical tape. A day or two, and it would be good as new. He even allowed her to put on a robe—a silky thing of dark blue that perfectly matched her eyes.

Though it was still early, the smell of the brewing coffee had awakened his appetite. "Let's eat something," he suggested. His arm around her shoulder, he led her to the kitchen, where Alana knelt on the floor beside the table without being directed to do so.

Mark popped some toast into the toaster and got out the butter and jam for the table, along with cream and sugar. He enjoyed doing things for his slave girl, though eventually, when she was fully acclimated to their lifestyle, he would have her wait on him, and take over basic cleaning duties.

"I got fresh strawberries yesterday at the market," he told her happily, as he washed them and brought them to the table. He selected one, cut off the leafy top and held it to her lips.

Alana took the fruit and slowly chewed. He loved to watch her sensual mouth move as she ate. He fed her another, and another, until the toast popped. As they ate their toast and sipped coffee, his heart filled, and he very nearly blurted the words he thought a dozen times, a thousand times, a day.

I love you, Alana.

But no. He couldn't say that to her. Though she was increasingly obedient and compliant, he knew she despised him. She didn't understand the true passion he offered, or the powerful elixir of a pure exchange of power. He had yanked her from a busy, stressful life, but also one of glamour and fame. He hoped she'd eventually come to love him and what he offered. For now, her obedience was enough.

He realized she was watching him through those long, thick lashes, her eyes directly on his face. He lifted his eyebrows in question, and she cleared her throat. "Excuse me, Sir," she said. "May I say something?"

"Yes? What is it?" His heart had absurdly begun to pound. Had he been wrong? Had love blossomed amidst the fear and struggle? Did she understand at last the potential of what they could share?

"How long are you going to keep me here?"

Disappointment rose like a hard lump in Mark's throat, which he tried desperately to swallow. What an idiot he'd been to let his hopes soar, even for a second. He had planned for two long years to abduct her. He had used his considerable brainpower and ingenuity to track her every move and determine the best way to steal her away from the world, but now that he had her, what had he truly expected would happen?

Somehow his dreams had included a happily-ever-after, but as he sat looking down at her, he was faced with the stark reality that would likely never happen. A rush of rage washed through him, scorching his consciousness like acid. Why couldn't she understand that what he'd done, he'd done for *them*?

Alana must have seen the change in his expression as he struggled to control his anger.

"Please," she said nervously. "Please, I'm sorry. Don't be angry."

He dispensed a forgiving backhand wave as he quashed both his anger and disappointment. "In answer to your question, I'll keep you as long as I like." He pushed back the chair and got to his feet. "Permission to speak is now over."

He couldn't have her love, but he certainly could have her body and her obedience. "Your punishment last night was aborted by your failure to stay in position. We'll finish now where we left off."

Her eyes widened in fear, her breath catching at his pronouncement. Good. She was right to be afraid.

"Since you're not yet properly trained, this time I'll restrain you more thoroughly so you can't move." Pulling her to her feet, Mark led the now trembling young woman to the playroom. He stripped her of her robe and attached the heavy metal collar around her neck. Leading her to the St. Andrew's cross, he positioned her so she was facing the cross. "Raise your arms and spread your legs," he instructed. He clipped her bracelets in place and, for good measure, he added the belt restraint at her waist. This time, he would leave her mouth free. He wanted to hear her cries.

He went to the rack and retrieved a longer, thinner cane than the one he'd used the night before. He returned to her and stopped short, still in awe of her gorgeous ass. He loved the two dimples, one above each perfectly rounded buttock.

He blew out a long breath. It wasn't fair to be angry with Alana because she didn't love him. He knew rationally there was no reason she should love him. *Patience*, he reminded himself. *Give her more time.* These thoughts calmed him somewhat, easing the ache in his heart.

"I'm going to give you twenty strokes," he announced. "Your job is to take your punishment with stoic grace. You may scream. You may cry, but you may not ask me to stop. When I'm done, you will thank me. Is your assignment clear?"

"Please, Sir" she begged, twisting back her head to catch his eye. "Please don't —"

"Silence," he boomed, irritation easier to handle than regret. "You protest again and I'll gag you and give you fifty."

She sucked in her breath and turned her head back to the front, her body sagging in defeat.

"We begin," he announced. "You will count aloud for me." The cane sliced through the air with a whoosh. It landed perfectly, just above one of the welts he'd painted there a few hours earlier.

"One," she yelped. Good girl.

He placed another just below the swell of her ass, across her slender thighs.

"Two! Ah, god, that hurts," Alana wailed.

Again and again he marked her, reaching in from time to time to run his finger along a rising welt, or place his hand between her legs to feel her heat. After the tenth stroke of the cane, she stopped wailing, her ragged breathing slowing to something deeper and more accepting. When he hit her for the eleventh time, something in her tone changed as she breathed the word. The sound was low and sensual in her throat, almost as if the cane were arousing her.

Thrilled and intrigued, Mark continued to punish his beautiful slave girl, his cock poking through the fly of his pajama bottoms and pointing straight at her all the while. When she finally sobbed the final count, he dropped the cane and yanked his pants from his body.

Moving close, he pressed himself against her heated ass. Instead of flinching or crying out, she only moaned, the sound like fingers cradling his shaft. Quickly, he released her from the cross and took her into his arms. He carried her to the soft lamb's wool throw rug in the corner of the playroom and set her down on her hands and knees.

"Stay up like that," he instructed. "I'm going to reward you with my cock." Crouching behind her, he draped himself over her, using one hand to guide his cock between her legs.

To his delighted shock, his shaft slid easily inside. She was wet! She wanted him, or at least what he was offering. Thrilled, he began to move, thrusting in and out of her perfect, tight cunt as he whispered her name over and over like a mantra, like a prayer.

~*~

What's happening to me?

Alana lay on her stomach on the soft rug, exhausted but also, and this was the strange part, curiously at peace. Something had happened while he was caning her. First there had been terror and pain, yes, but as he'd hit her again and again, something had shifted inside her, the fear bleeding away, replaced with something that wasn't quite pleasure, but something darker and more complex.

When he'd taken her down and entered her from behind, for the first time his large, hard cock hadn't hurt her—hadn't torn the sensitive flesh at her entrance. Instead, it had felt good going in, and even better as he'd filled her, his hands on her hips, pulling her back into him with each thrust. Though she couldn't come from that angle without direct stimulation to her clit, she'd experienced the warm, buttery feeling of sexual pleasure, pleasure that could lead to orgasm with just a touch of his fingers, the press of his lips, the stroke of his tongue…

She lifted her head and looked around the

strange, empty room — painted white from ceiling to floor, what the hell was that about? The sun was just rising, the room bathed in a pearly gray light that outlined the scary torture devices set around the space like some kind of stage set for a medieval film. Except this wasn't a stage — it was all too real. And he wasn't her lover — he was her captor, her tormentor, her *Master*…

After he'd climaxed, he'd lifted himself from her body and left the room. Where was he now? Had he gone back to sleep? Was he locked in his study clicking away on his computer? What if she made a run for it?

Slowly, she hoisted herself to her feet. Her ass and the backs of her thighs were stinging. She winced as she reached back to gingerly touch one of the raised welts. Did she dare try to find some clothing? Or should she just make her break and take her chances?

Cautiously, she walked to the dungeon door and placed her hand on the knob. She turned it slowly and gently pulled.

It was locked.

Chapter 6

The weeks edged into a month, and they were happy as two lovebirds in their private nest—at least he was. He loved to walk into the playroom and see her bound and suspended from the overhead bar he'd so cleverly rigged. She waited for him with her feet barely touching the ground, arms spread in welcome for him like a gift, like a prize.

He liked to leave her a while, trembling with anticipation as he went about a task or two at his computer or puttered around their cozy farmhouse. Upon returning to the playroom, he invariably experienced a split second of joyous surprise—how had this gorgeous woman come to be tethered in his dungeon, naked and waiting just for him?

He stroked his cock as he imagined Alana at his feet, his cock down her throat.

She was doing well with her deep-throat technique, thanks to his patient lessons. He liked to start out by having her kneel at his feet. He would sit on the bed just in front of her and lean forward, slapping her cheeks with the side of his erect cock. There was something so deliciously humiliating in the act, and he never tired of her startled expression when his cock made contact with her face.

Once she was able to take it with, if not grace, at least stoicism, he would inform her she had now earned the right to worship his cock.

She had learned that was her cue to obediently part her luscious lips, just as she did when he fed her. Holding her head still with his hands, he would guide his erect shaft into her mouth, moving slowly forward until the tip touched the back of her throat.

The first few sessions when he'd done this, she'd gagged and tried to pull away. But a swift slap to the face reminded her more readily than any admonition to stay still and take it. Eventually, she had learned to accommodate his substantial girth, and now, though her eyes might water, her face turning red when he blocked her windpipe, the obedient slut no longer pulled away.

He would press forward until her nose was touching his pubic bone. When her eyes began to bulge, and only then, he would ease back to allow her to gasp for air, but only for a few seconds. Then he would ease himself back into the sweet, wet heat of her mouth, not stopping until the tip was again lodged against the soft tissue at the back of her throat.

How easy it would be to kill someone this way — to suffocate them with your cock. Of course, they would have to acquiesce, to stay still while you slowly shut down their brain and ultimately their heart. Not that Mark would ever do that. He wanted Alana alive. Without her, he would be nothing.

Aware he'd completely lost his thread of concentration, Mark shut down the computer and pushed back from his desk. Alana was waiting for him. He didn't want to disappoint her.

As he entered the playroom, he whistled with appreciation. Alana was perfect — her arms high overhead, her legs cuffed on either side of the metal spreader bar that would hold her still, no matter what he did to her. She glanced up at him as he entered. She looked down quickly, as befitted a proper slave girl.

She no longer pleaded to be set free.

Perhaps she was finally accepting that this life was now her lot, her freedom. He had set her free from the incredible stress and clamor of her days as a movie star and sought-after celebrity. Now all she had to focus on was him.

Mark approached Alana and kissed her on the mouth, wishing for an instant that she'd kiss him back. Maybe one day…

He took a step back and smiled at her. "I just finished the code for a project that's going to make us very rich. In celebration, it's time we focused more on your sexual training. You're becoming an obedient submissive, but you're not yet properly sexualized."

He stripped out of his clothing, leaving them in a pile near the door. He went to the high narrow table he'd placed beside her. He surveyed the array of phalluses he'd arranged there just for her, along with a fresh tube of lubricant and a gleaming pair of clover nipple clamps. No doubt she'd been staring at the toys while waiting for his return.

He picked up a large, rubbery flesh-colored phallus that resembled a real penis, right down to veins on the thick shaft. "Today is your first day of dildo training. Does that please you, cunt girl?"

From the expression on her face, she clearly was not pleased, and he was mildly amused as he watched her press her lips together in an obvious attempt not to say something she would regret.

Still, he had asked a direct question, and he expected an answer. He set down the lifelike cock and approached her.

Grasping a handful of her silky hair, he jerked her head back. "I asked you a question."

"If it would please you, Sir," she said through clenched teeth.

Mark nodded, releasing her hair. The words were correct, even if the sincerity was lacking. No matter, he was satisfied with the response. "It does."

He picked up the black rubber penis gag, basically a ball gag in the shape of a small penis. "Open wide," he said with an evil grin as he brought it to her mouth.

Instead, it was her eyes that widened as she took in the diabolical device. "No, please," she began, but he cut her off by pushing the shaft into her mouth.

"Yes, please," he replied. "I like the idea of filling all your holes with cock today." She gagged and sputtered as he positioned the gag, but bound as she was, she couldn't get away. He buckled the gag around her head and took a step back to admire her. She looked so helpless with the penis gag down her throat, the small balls protruding between her teeth. He regarded her a moment to make sure she could breathe. By the slight flare of her nostrils and the rise and fall of her chest, he was satisfied that she could.

Next, he showed her the butt plug, and he could tell from her expression she knew exactly what it was, and didn't like it one bit. "Do you like anal play?" he asked teasingly. "Do you like a big, hard dick shoved up your ass, slave girl?"

She vehemently shook her head, emitting a gurgled cry of obvious distress. Her entire body tensed as she tried to move in her chains, but all she could manage was the slightest twist.

Mark's cock hardened further at her delightful reaction, which he was sure wasn't feigned. She really was terrified of a little butt plug. His darling girl must be an anal virgin, and the realization thrilled him. He'd been so busy exploring and torturing the rest of that luscious body, he'd neglected her pretty little asshole. Today, he would remedy that, and then some.

He squeezed a small dollop of lubricant on his index finger and moved behind her. She jerked as he rimmed her tiny, tight opening with his gooey finger. She yelped against her cock gag as he pushed it inside. He moved his finger until he felt the muscles relax a little. Withdrawing his finger, he reached for the butt plug.

He squirted more lubricating jelly over its head and pressed the tip between her spread cheeks. She tried to twist back her head, no doubt to plead with her eyes, but bound as she was, she couldn't quite manage it.

Ignoring her silent protest, Mark pushed the plug slowly but surely into her tight passage. "Relax," he urged. "It'll be easier for you if you can relax." He chuckled. "I had no idea you were an anal virgin, sweetheart. It will truly be my honor to pluck that particular cherry."

She was breathing hard through her nose now, her chest heaving, and as he seated the flared base, she squealed against her gag, her entire body going momentarily rigid.

Mark tugged lightly at the soft circle of rubbery plastic at the base of the plug, satisfied that her sphincter muscles would keep it in place until he was ready to remove it. "There, you see?" he said, leaning forward to kiss her soft cheek. "You did it. Good girl. You took the plug all the way in. It'll open you up nicely for when I fuck your ass with my big, hard dick." He stroked his erect shaft in anticipation, but first he had other tortures in mind.

He pushed back her heavy hair and kissed her on the neck. She was sweating, a pulse jumping at her throat. "One day," he whispered in her ear, "you'll beg me for it. You'll kneel and spread your ass for me, and you'll beg, 'Please, Sir. Please fuck me in the ass.'"

He returned to the table and picked up the large penis-shaped dildo. As he turned back to his darling girl, she pleaded mutely with her eyes. Was she begging for it, the little slut? With a laugh, he chose to assume she was. "That's right, my little slut. I know you want me to fuck you with this big, hard cock. They say size doesn't matter, but we both know that's a crock, don't we?"

She didn't nod in agreement, but he decided the question was rhetorical, and so he'd give her a pass. He lubricated the huge phallus and placed it between Alana's perfect breasts. Dragging the tip along her skin, he drew it down her belly to her cunt, spread wide by the bar between her legs. Slowly, sensually, he used the tip to stroke her labia and moved it gently, teasingly, over her clit. He nudged the head of the dildo at her entrance and pushed it an inch or so inside her.

She grunted behind the gag. He alternated between teasing her clit and easing the large phallus inside her, a little more each time. Her grunting had quieted, her body relaxing somewhat in her bonds.

He pulled away the dildo for a moment so he could cup her hot pussy in his hand. He inserted a finger deep inside her, delighted by what he found. "Wet!" he crowed triumphantly. "My whore is wet!" He peered into her lovely face. "You want this. You need what I'm giving you."

He again pressed the rubber cock slowly inside her, this time pushing it farther than he yet had. It was huge, but slowly, carefully, he worked it deeper and deeper into her hot, tight cunt. He watched her face as he invaded her body. At first her eyes were squeezed shut, her nose wrinkled, but as he slowly, sensually worked the shaft inside her, her eyelids relaxed, though they remained closed, her scrunched face easing. Her cheeks and throat were flushed, her nipples erect, and he could smell the intoxicating scent of her juices, which now coated the lucky phallus.

He wanted to hear her come, and so he unbuckled and removed the penis gag. She gasped for breath as he wiped away the drool from her chin. Again positioning the phallus at her cunt, he pushed it deep inside her in one, smooth thrust.

Alana moaned, a low guttural sound, and he could feel the clench of her vaginal muscles against the invading object. He allowed it to slide out several inches and thrust it back, pressing even deeper this time. She groaned, a small shudder moving through her taut frame.

Excited, he began to fuck her with the rubber cock, moving in and out of her slick embrace until she was panting, her lips parted and glistening. Clearly there was pleasure here. Now he just needed to add some pain.

"Remember," he murmured, as he withdrew the shaft with a soft popping sound and placed it on the supply table. "With the pleasure, must come the pain. The two are inextricably bound for you, my love. You serve me through their combination."

Her eyes opened wide, fear replacing the pleasure that had suffused her face a moment before.

His cock throbbing, Mark reached for the nipple clamps. Grabbing one perfect gumdrop nipple, he twisted and rolled it between his forefinger and thumb and pulled it taut. Pressing open one of the clamps, he let it close against the base of her nipple.

Predictably, Alana screamed.

He did the same with the other nipple, drawing another cry from his girl. He took a step back to admire his handiwork. The clamp chain hung prettily between her high, round breasts.

Alana was breathing very fast, to the point of hyperventilating. Cupping his hand gently over her mouth and nose, Mark said soothingly, "Slow down your breathing. Take it easy. Your body will adjust to the tension. You've taken much worse than this, my brave darling."

Removing his hand, he smoothed her wild hair from her face as her breathing slowly eased to something approaching normal.

He picked up the rubber cock and squirted a touch more lube over its crown. Positioning himself again in front of her, he stroked her labia and clit with the fat head until she began to breathe more deeply, a sure sign of her arousal. Satisfied, he slowly pushed the dildo inside her.

As he began to fuck her with the phallus, her breath quickened, her hips moving in time with the thrusts. He loved watching the chain jiggle between her clamped nipples as he fucked her, hard and fast now, with the faux cock.

"Oh, god," she finally moaned, her body trembling.

"Don't forget," he warned her.

"May I—" She couldn't seem to get the words out. She gasped as he relentlessly thrust the cock in and out of her slick, gaping cunt.

"Oh, god," she breathed again. "Please. May I come…" The last word was drawn out and ended in a rising scream.

"Yes," he assented, his voice hoarse with lust. "Come for me, you slut."

Jerking hard in her restraints, the chain whipping wildly between her breasts, Alana climaxed with a long, high-pitched wail.

Mark watched, entranced, his hand moving furiously over his own cock now, unable to hold on for another second. In less than a minute, he sent long ribbons of hot ejaculate over her belly and thighs, his pleasure yanked from his body as he groaned with deep satisfaction.

~*~

Alana drifted a moment in the aftermath of the powerful climax, the endorphins from the orgasm sending waves of warm pleasure through her body. After a while, discomfort began to intrude on the pleasure. Her nipples and her arms were numb, and her ankles were chafed from the slave bracelets rubbing against the cuffs of the spreader bar. She longed to close her legs, to lie down and wrap her arms around her body as she curled into a tight, protected ball.

She opened her eyes slowly, focusing on the tall, naked man standing in front of her, his spent cock still fisted in his hand, his blond hair flopping over his forehead and into his green-gold eyes.

Dimly, she recalled the before time, when she'd been surrounded by friends and lovers, but she let the memories slide away. It was easier just to forget. Mark was all that existed now. He was the man, the Master, who gave her food, or withheld it. The man who would force her into the punishment cage, or take her lovingly into his bed. The man who gave her incredible sexual pleasure — pleasure she'd never known with another person — but always at a steep price.

The bondage, clamps and the anal plug were not enough of a price for the orgasm — she knew that. For each pound of pleasure, he would exact at least two of pain. In a peculiar way, she almost looked forward to it. Because once he hurt her, then he would let her down. He would bathe her and soothe her and hold her tenderly in his arms.

It was all so confusing, and she was tired. She longed to be released from the suspension rack, but she knew better than to ask. In order to survive, she'd learned silence and obedience in her time here. How long had it been? Days, weeks, months? She had no idea. Time had lost its meaning, reduced to small blocks of pleasure, pain, deprivation, fear, tenderness.

So confusing…

Give me the pain, so I can rest, she telegraphed to the Master.

He smiled slowly, a cruel lift of sensual lips, and she knew he'd heard her silent plea. He moved behind her and tugged lightly at the nasty plug he'd shoved into her ass.

Back in her other life, she'd never permitted anyone to touch her there — end of story. But that other life no longer existed.

Forget it. Let it go…

The thing had really hurt going in, especially that last flared bit, but then it had been okay. When he'd fucked her with that huge dildo, at first she'd thought he was going to split her in two, but then something wonderful had happened — the thick, hard fullness inside her had completely taken her over, pushing out all thoughts, fear and pain, replacing it with a dark, heady pleasure that produced a powerful, obliterating orgasm. That was the best — when the pleasure and the pain blocked out everything else — when she was fully in the moment, her mind blissfully shut down.

The plug eased out of her, and Mark appeared in her peripheral vision as he dropped the offending object into a bowl, no doubt for later cleaning. The thought made her blush with humiliation and for a moment, hatred pushed its way through her consciousness, but she shook it away. Hate was too exhausting, and only made her cry with frustration and fury.

Easier just to accept…

Mark reappeared in front of her. He tugged lightly at the chain between her breasts, awakening the sleeping nerve endings in her numbed nipples. "These have to come off, Alana. It's going to hurt, but only for a second."

Before she could react, he pressed on the sides of each clamp, releasing the tight mechanisms that held them in place.

The pain was blinding — a white-hot explosion of agony, and Alana screamed, tears springing to her eyes.

"Oh, poor baby. Let me distract you," Mark said in that silky, smooth tone that was at once seductive and sadistically evil, a sure signal the "distraction" would not be a pleasant one.

He picked up a riding crop from the umbrella stand he kept filled with crops, canes and whips, and brought it down hard against one tender nipple. Another explosion of raw pain hurtled through Alana's frame. He struck the second nipple, and then moved behind her. With a steady slapping of leather against skin, he painted her ass and the backs of her thighs with fire until she was crying, panting and begging him to stop.

He returned to stand in front of her and set the crop on the table nearby. Alana sagged with relief. It was nearly over.

He took her head between his hands and kissed her, his tongue moving in slow, sensual circles in her mouth and over her lips as he gently cradled her breasts and brushed her tender nipples with his thumbs.

Just as she was relaxing into the pleasure of his touch, he took a step back and reached for the crop once more. This time, he whipped it up sharply between her spread legs, the small square of leather making direct contact on her spread pussy.

Alana howled with pain.

He struck her again and again, until the tortured flesh began to numb. Then it began to happen. That thing — that secret, private thing she didn't understand, didn't know how to bring on, but which sometimes happened just when she didn't think she could take another stroke of pain.

It wasn't that he would stop what he was doing, but somehow her body began to process it differently. The pain shifted—not precisely into pleasure, but into something equally, if not more, powerful. When this happened, all panic and fear would ebb away, replaced by a deep, welcome sense of peace.

As he continued to strike her exposed, tender cunt, the peace settled over her like a warm, blanket, and she closed her eyes and let it take her…

"Yes, that's it, slave girl. That's it, my love. Surrender to the pain. Surrender to me." His voice was muted beneath the deep, slow pulse of her blood in her ears, but she sensed the praise in his voice, and she smiled.

The Master was pleased. That was good…

Then she felt his fingers stroking like velvet over her bruised labia and in circles around her swollen clit. Oh god, it felt good… so good…

"Please, Sir," she managed to whisper. "May I come?"

"Yes," he consented.

She did.

After rest and dinner, he brought her back to the dungeon. He was wearing a pair of black jeans, his large, thick cock already bulging beneath the denim, his muscular chest bare. He pointed his finger imperiously to the floor, and Alana lowered herself to her knees.

To her surprise, instead of telling her what he intended to do to her, he asked her. "Alana. What am I going to do to you tonight? What did I prepare you for earlier today?"

She had to think a moment. Then she remembered — all too well. She took a deep breath and let it out. "You are going to fuck me in the ass, Sir." Her sphincter muscles clenched and she bit her lower lip. The anal plug was one thing, but his cock was huge.

He smiled that cruel smile that always promised pain. "That's correct. I'm going to fuck you in that lovely, tight ass of yours. And what's more, you are going to beg me to do it, aren't you?"

There was only one answer to the question that wasn't really a question, but a command.

Alana licked her dry lips. "Yes Sir," she whispered, heat washing over her cheeks.

"Do it now. Beg me."

Alana worried her lower lip again as she forced herself to form the words. They were just words. Just words. "Please, Sir," she managed. "Please fuck your slave girl in the ass."

He smiled again, perfect white teeth in that handsome, cruel face. "It would be my pleasure, cunt." He unzipped his fly and pushed his jeans down his muscular legs. "But first, you'll suck my cock."

Alana leaned up dutifully, glad for this momentary reprieve. She had learned through daily practice to take her Master's cock deep into her throat. Sometimes he pushed it in so deep she couldn't breathe. He would hold her that way for ten, twenty, thirty seconds, sometimes longer. She never struggled anymore, never tried to pull away. In an odd way, she had come to welcome those little breaks from life, as she thought of them, especially when he held her so long that her mind shut itself down and she drifted...drifted...

She was returned to reality as he pulled his cock from her mouth and said, his voice hoarse with lust, "Get down on the mat, forehead on the floor, ass in the air. Reach back and spread your cheeks. I'm going to lube your virgin hole and fuck you. You will keep your ass cheeks spread until I slap your hands away. Got it?"

"Yes, Sir." Alana's heart had begun to beat too fast, a pulse ticking in her throat. She'd never, ever let any man near her ass, but then, Mark wasn't any man. He was her Master. She had no choice…

She positioned herself as ordered on the thick yoga mat and reached back to spread her cheeks, her face flaming. She heard him moving behind her, and a moment later, the cold shock of lubricant being smeared over her puckered hole.

He crouched behind her. She felt his finger invade her, and then the nudge of his fat cockhead, mercifully gooey with lube.

"Ask me to do it to you," he ordered.

Her voice trembling slightly, she made herself say, "Please Sir. Please fuck me in the ass." She slowed her breathing in a conscious effort to relax and accept the cock that was going to take her one way or the other.

He pushed lightly between her cheeks. "Beg me."

"Please, Sir," she repeated, trying to put more

fervor into it. Her voice came out raspy and she cleared her throat. "Please, Mark, fuck me in the ass."

"Do you want it, cunt?"

No.

"Yes. Yes, please, Sir. I want it."

He laughed with delight. "Then you shall have it." He pressed harder against her asshole, pushing past the tight ring of muscle. A small, sharp burst of pain radiated through her anus, and Alana tensed, crying out.

"Relax," he commanded, pushing harder. He slapped her hands away. Hard fingers gripped her hips as he guided himself into her.

"It hurts, it hurts, it hurts," she moaned, jerked reflexively forward.

His fingers dug into her hips as he continued to push himself deeper inside her. "Only because you aren't giving yourself fully to me. You're resisting. You begged me for this, slave girl. Now take what I give you."

Alana was panting, but the pain, she was forced to acknowledge, had eased somewhat, replaced by a sense of fullness that was uncomfortable, but manageable.

"That's right," Mark soothed, reaching forward to stroke her hair back from her face. "Much better. I'm almost all the way in now, and it feels fucking amazing. You're so tight, so perfect." He thrust forward again, harder than before, and Alana grunted with the force of it.

Then, to her surprise, he reached around her body with one hand and began to fondle her pussy with lubricated fingers. Alana focused on the pleasure, gathering it up and holding it close as he began to fuck her hard from behind.

As he teased her, the fullness inside her ass eased into something almost pleasurable, and his fingers moving expertly over her pussy were bringing her rapidly to a climax. As her anal muscles fully relaxed, his huge cock actually felt good moving inside her. His hand at her sex felt better than good.

"Please, Sir," she gasped. "May I come?"

"You may, cunt." He continued his finger dance on her pussy. His hand fell away as he groaned, low and feral. He slammed into her with ferocious force. His body shuddered in a series of small, powerful spasms. He fell heavily against her, his weight causing her to collapse beneath him, his cock still buried deep in her ass.

The anal virgin was a virgin no more.

Chapter 7

The mysterious disappearance of Alana Hunter was still occasionally in the news. The police still claimed to be exploring "promising leads."

For all intents and purposes, she no longer existed for the outside world. But she was everything to Mark, and he gave her everything she needed.

He was very pleased with her progress. She was a perfect slut when it came to giving head, and she had learned to take a whipping with real grace. She never asked anymore when he would let her go. She no longer begged to be set free. She dropped obediently to the floor when he touched her shoulder. She knew never to sit on the furniture. She rarely expressed any discomfort, even when he left her tightly bound for long periods of time.

Lately, when he left the house to run errands, he enjoyed tying her to a low stool, just inside the front door with her back facing the door. She would drape herself on her stomach over the stool, legs spread wide, so when he opened the door, the first thing he saw was that gorgeous ass and spread pussy.

Sometimes before he left, he would stick a dildo in her cunt, or an anal plug in her ass. Sometimes both. He would warn her they had better be in place when he returned or she would suffer the consequences. She usually managed to keep them in, but one afternoon when Mark returned, his arms full of groceries, he saw that the dildo had slipped out of her cunt onto the floor. Alana, being tied tightly by her wrists and ankles to the stool, had been powerless to retrieve it.

"Oh dear," he said, setting down his bags and coming to stand behind her. "My naughty slut pushed out the dildo. What happens to naughty sluts who disobey?"

"They get punished, Sir," she said in a small voice.

"That's right," he agreed pleasantly. "Shall I cane you? Or do you want to be flogged?"

Still bound to the stool, Alana whispered, "The flogger, please, Sir."

"Hmm." He pretended to ponder, having known she would go for the less painful option. "I don't think so. Your welts from the other day are fading. I want to see some fresh stripes on that luscious ass."

He selected a long, whippy cane from the umbrella stand he kept just inside the front door for precisely this purpose. He stepped around in front of the bound girl and held the cane to her lips. "Kiss it," he commanded.

She kissed it. Lifting her head as best as she was able, she pleaded, "Please, Sir. I'm sorry the dildo fell out. I tried my best, I promise. I—"

"Your best wasn't good enough today. I know you're sorry, but you still have to be punished. You do want the cane, don't you?"

"I…" She trailed off. "If it pleases you, Sir."

"No, I'm asking if *you* want it. You know you displeased your Master by failing to obey my command. You know you deserve to be punished, but do you *want* it? Answer yes or no."

He waited while she struggled for the correct response. Of course, there was only one response available to her. She was forbidden the luxury of refusal. She knew that, knew it only too well. But the cane was the one thing she had yet to fully accept. She had continued to resist him, still terrified by its wicked cut, even though he'd only drawn blood once, and that time by accident.

He prodded her side gently with his foot. In a kind voice that belied his sadistic intent, he said, "Answer me. Do you want to be caned by your Master? Yes or no?"

"Yes," she finally whispered.

Thrilled, Mark replied, "Good girl. Yes, you want it. You want it because I want it. That's all you have to know. Ever." He bent down, drawing the stiff rod across her bare back. She flinched but, of course, could not get away.

"There, now, my love," Mark crooned. "It's not as if you didn't earn this. You brought this entirely on yourself with your lack of control. Now take it bravely and it will be over before you know it."

He brought the cane down on her offered ass, catching both cheeks at once, painting a white line that quickly darkened to red.

Alana screamed, her hands clenching into tight fists above her cuffs.

He whipped the cane against the backs of her thighs, and added a few more welts on her ass. The last one he aimed vertically across her bared, spread cunt and asshole. The stroke was lighter, of course, but hard enough to produce a long, loud wail that didn't stop for several seconds.

Satisfied, Mark left her bound to the stool while he went to put away the groceries. When he released her from the stool, he pushed her to her knees in front of him. Pulling out his rigid cock, he forced it between her lips. Taking her head in his hands, he thrust in and out of her open mouth with long, smooth strokes until he spurted down her throat. Tucking his cock back into his jeans, he wiped away her tears with his thumb and patted her on the head. "Go freshen up. I'll make us some dinner."

After dinner, they watched a football game on TV. Mark wasn't really paying too much attention to the game, distracted as he was by his footrest. Alana was on her hands and knees in front of him, her back supporting his feet. Her breasts hung down like delicious fruit begging to be plucked and suckled. Her ass cheeks were pleasingly splayed, revealing the sweetly pouting pussy lips between her legs. Christ, she was perfect.

Mark finished his first beer and reached for another from the small cooler he'd brought from the kitchen. He popped it, took a long drink, and set it on her back. "Make sure you don't spill it, slave," he warned her.

She'd only been down there for maybe thirty minutes when she shifted her weight, almost upsetting the beer near his right foot. "Whoa," Mark said sharply. "Watch yourself."

"Please, Sir," she whined. "I'm feeling very stiff. My knees hurt."

Mark pursed his lips. "If I let you up, you'll have to pay the price for failing to be my proper footrest. It's your choice. Endure a little longer, or take your just punishment." His cock hardened with anticipation as he waited for her to choose.

Alana fell silent, apparently weighing the unfair choice offered her. She managed to stay still for another twenty minutes or so, but eventually she began to tremble as her muscles strained to support her. His beer can wobbled.

"Sir?"

"Yes?"

"I can't. I'm sorry, but I can't."

All at once, her arms gave out and Alana fell to the ground, the beer can falling with her, spilling into her hair and onto the nice carpet. Alana lay in a heap, too exhausted even to wipe the beer away.

"Get up," Mark commanded sternly. He stood, nudging her side with his foot.

Alana made an effort to rise, but fell back down, clearly exhausted. He almost felt sorry for her.

Mark lifted the girl to her feet, and into his arms. "I was just about to let you up," he lied. "Now you'll have to pay the price."

He strode to the bathroom and lay Alana into the empty tub.

She shivered as her body touched the cold porcelain, and fixed him with those beautiful, deep blue eyes. "Please, Sir, I'm sorry, Sir. Please have mercy, Sir," she begged, her voice trembling.

"Mercy?" Mark lifted his eyebrows. "For what? You can't even hold a position and I should show you mercy? You weren't being whipped. You weren't being tortured. All you had to do was kneel there, and you failed. Clearly, you need stamina training. We'll start that tomorrow. Meanwhile, since you've already got half that beer slopped all over you, I'll go ahead and give you the rest of it."

At first Alana looked confused, as he hadn't brought what remained of the beer into the bathroom. His meaning became clear as he unzipped his pants and pulled out his semi-erect penis. The look of barely contained horror on her face was priceless, but she wisely refrained from protest.

Standing close to the edge of the tub he directed, "Since you did such a lousy job being my table, now you'll be my toilet. Spread your legs wide. I'm going to piss on your cunt."

To his annoyed surprise, she didn't immediately obey.

"Do it, Alana." Mark's voice was steely. "Do it or I'll put you in the cage and piss on you there."

That got her attention, and Alana quickly spread her legs. Because of her disobedience, he decided to add insult to injury. "Spread your cunt open for me. And raise your hips in the air so I can piss right on your clit."

Alana did as he ordered, a blush spreading up her chest all the way to the tops of her ears.

With a grin, Mark began to piss on her spread sex. Alana turned her head away as the warm stream sprayed across her clit, her belly and her thighs. He had a hard time finishing, because his cock got so hard at the sight of his humiliated slave girl succumbing to his perverse whims.

Next time he would piss in her mouth.

When he was done, he started to zip up, but had another idea. "Kneel up in the bathtub and suck me off, slave."

Alana looked dismayed. "But Sir! I'm covered in — I'm a mess. Please let me wash off first, Sir?"

Mark regarded his bedraggled slave girl. How marvelous that this gorgeous, famous actress, who wouldn't have given him the time of day back in her former life, was kneeling naked in his tub, covered in piss and beer, begging for mercy. His cock was now hard as a bar of iron. A drop of piss dangled at its tip, but he didn't shake it off.

"You heard me, cunt. Get over here and suck me off, before I really get angry."

She lowered her head like a good, obedient slave girl and lifted herself as ordered. She opened her mouth, reaching out to cup his balls as he'd taught her, but he stopped her. "Hands behind your back."

Alana dutifully clasped her hands behind her back and leaned forward, her mouth open, lips parted to receive his offering.

Mark grabbed her head and fucked her face, hard and fast. He was pleased she kept her hands behind her back, one hand firmly clasping each elbow, as he had taught her to do. He liked the way her breasts jutted forward when she did that. God, she was sexy, even covered in beer and piss. He pulled her forward, coming deep into her throat.

He pushed her from him, so that she fell back, sprawling against the far side of the bathtub. Mark tucked his now spent cock back into his pants. With a deeply satisfied sigh, he said, "Get yourself cleaned up. I'm going to watch the rest of the game."

No question about it. Life was good.

The sun was just setting, the late November sky darkening to purple. There was a chill in the air, despite the efforts of the old baseboard heating system, and Mark decided to build a fire.

Alana was kneeling obediently by the couch in front of the old stone fireplace, watching as he opened the flue and lit a match to the kindling he'd strategically placed around the logs.

Soon he had a fire crackling in the grate. The scene was cozy, and as he took his seat on the couch, he reached out his arms, feeling suddenly magnanimous toward his obedient slave girl. She stared at him, a question on her face, so he explained, "Come on up here on the couch. You've been such a good girl, and I want to hold you in my arms."

She smiled — an actual, genuine smile — perhaps the first smile he'd seen since that day months ago when she'd climbed into the back seat of the sedan. His heart rose in his throat at that smile, and for the first time, a small but persistent voice from somewhere deep inside him demanded, *"What the hell have you done to this woman? How dare you take such full possession of another person's life?"*

The voice irritated him, and he quickly shoved it back down, calmed as she climbed up onto the couch and allowed him to take her into his arms. Her smile faded as he pulled her close, but she snuggled docilely against him, her eyes closed. She belonged to him now. There was no going back. He leaned down proprietarily, kissing the top of her head, confident she would do anything he asked of her now — anything at all.

A light snow had begun to fall outside the window in the deepening twilight. Mark glanced down at his naked slave, his cock rising with a sudden sadistic idea. How far was Alana truly willing to suffer for him?

Not that she had a choice. It was the grace with

which she accepted his devised tortures that attracted him. Submission with grace could almost equal love, he told himself.

"Alana," he said, dropping his arm from around her shoulders and turning to face her. "Let's go outside."

"Outside?" she repeated stupidly, though he could understand her confusion. In the months since he'd saved her, she hadn't left the confines of his house, not even to step into the fenced-in backyard.

"Yes," he said, getting to his feet and pulling her upright. "It's the first snow. I always love the first snow, don't you?"

"Yes, Sir," she agreed, her face suddenly alight with expectation.

He led her to the bedroom, where he pulled on corduroy pants, a long-sleeved undershirt and a thick pullover sweater.

Alana, waiting on her knees, said finally, "Excuse me, Sir. May I speak?"

"You may." Mark sat on the edge of the bed to pull on his socks and boots.

"May I dress myself, Sir? To go outside, I

mean." She was, of course, aware of the clothing he'd bought for her, as it hung on one of the racks in the closet where he still sometimes confined her to the cage when she was naughty. He'd taken to keeping her naked all the time, however, seeing no point in covering all that beauty, even for a second.

"Hmm," he said slowly, as if considering the question. "No, I don't think so. We'll just be in the backyard. You'll be fine as you are."

She looked confused. "But it's cold and —" she began, but he cut her off.

"Do you have a problem with that, cunt girl?" He hadn't called her that in a while, and she knew it signaled his displeasure.

Abruptly, she pressed her lips together, her face coloring as she wrapped her arms around her torso.

"I asked you a question, cunt girl."

"No Sir," she whispered, aware that was the only correct response.

Mark's cock hardened with sadistic anticipation. This was going to be fun.

He decided to let her wear the pair of rain boots he kept by the back door. Even in oversized, black rubber boots, she still looked sexy as hell.

He led her out the back door to the secluded backyard. The snow had stopped, and the first few stars were starting to prick the sky. Though he didn't feel cold at all, their breath was visible on the air. Alana wrapped her arms around her naked body and shivered, but she didn't complain.

Mark led her to the shed at the back of the yard. He retrieved the key from beneath some old bricks on the side of the building, and opened the padlock that held the doors closed. Taking several coils of rope from wall hooks, he handed them to Alana. "Carry these and follow me," he instructed.

He had her stop between two trees that were spaced about five feet apart. "Spread your legs and hold out your arms like a human X," he told her. He waited until she obeyed. Then he quickly and expertly tied slipknots around her thighs and wrists, and pulled the ropes tight, wrapping them around each fat trunk.

He stepped back, thrilled by the sight. Alana's nipples were like hard little marbles in the puckered circles of her areolas. She was shivering, her skin flushed pink in its effort to warm itself. But not one word of protest had been uttered, not one entreaty.

"God, you're gorgeous," he breathed. "You need to be punished, just for being so fucking beautiful." Yes. She did need it. And he would oblige.

Mark ran back to the house and returned with a heavy flogger. Slowly, sensually, he began to caress her body with the leather thongs, warming her flesh with each stroke. Gradually he built up the intensity until she began to gasp and pant, her breath rasping in her throat. He covered her body, moving around the trees so he could focus first on her back, then on her front, whipping her flesh with the soft leather until she was jerking and writhing in her restraints, gasping and crying out when the tips of leather caught her across the nipple, or between her spread legs.

"Go ahead, darling," he urged, thrilled. "Scream as loud as you like. No one will hear you. No one will see you. No one will save you."

He whipped her hard. He wanted to make her scream, to shatter this new-found grace she seemed to have acquired. It would never be enough. No matter how much she took, he wanted her to take more. He would build her up and break her down, again and again and again.

He whipped her until his arm was tired. Alana was crying softly, her body ablaze from the beating. Her head hung forward, her long, dark hair obscuring her face. Even in the cold night air, she was wet with sweat.

Dropping the flogger in what was left of the snow, Mark bent down to release the ropes around her thighs, leaving her arms still shackled between the trees. He unzipped his pants and moved forward to embrace the naked woman. Lifting her up onto his hips, Mark nudged his cock against her perfect cunt. As she dropped her head against his shoulder, he pushed forward, delighted as his cock slid easily inside her.

She could cry and moan all she liked, but the slut was wet from her beating. He groaned with pleasure as her hot, wet cunt sheathed his cock like a velvet glove. The pleasure was so intense he could have come with only a few thrusts, but he desperately wanted to prolong this delicious, exquisite moment.

Slowing his pace, he cupped her ass, squeezing the heated, tender flesh as he eased his cock in and out of her pussy. "Fuck," he breathed. "It's just too damn good." He gave up the fight and ejaculated, pumping hard into her tight cunt.

Balancing her on his hips, his cock still inside her, Mark released her wrists from the rope, and carried the limp, shivering young woman into the house. He laid her gently on the couch and pulled off her boots.

She didn't move, though she followed him with her eyes.

He stoked the fire, adding more wood to the blaze. Sitting beside her, he rubbed a soothing salve into her tender, welted flesh. Despite the heat in the room, her skin remained cold to the touch.

He pulled the throw from the back of the couch and wrapped her in its soft folds. Then he settled her on his lap, holding her tightly until she finally stopped shivering.

The inviting smell of the beef stew he'd made in the crockpot earlier that afternoon permeated the room, and Mark realized he was hungry.

After dinner, he decided to open a bottle of champagne. A delightfully cruel idea was hatching in his head. Alana peed for him now without embarrassment. It was accepted as a matter of course. How could he heighten her sense of submission regarding this natural bodily function?

Until now, every time she had asked to relieve herself, he had allowed it. But tonight, he thought as he filled her fluted glass with the fine, dry champagne, would be a different story.

"You may hold the glass, sweetheart." Mark

offered no explanation for the extra bit of independence. He didn't usually allow Alana to hold anything. He liked to control every aspect of her eating and drinking, but he reasoned she would probably drink more if she had control of the glass, and he planned to make sure she had plenty.

His plan worked, and she drank two glasses in quick succession. But when he attempted to pour her a third, she shook her head. "Please, Sir," she said. "I think I've had enough. I'll get drunk."

"So you get drunk. So what? I bet you're cute when you're drunk." He took the glass from her and filled it. Holding it to her lips, he forced her to take a sip. At his insistence, Alana drank the rest of the glass.

All that champagne on top of the water with dinner would definitely do the trick. He led her back to the living room and sat on the couch, using Alana as a footrest while he contemplated the dying fire in the hearth. Not more than twenty minutes passed before she said, "Excuse me, Sir. May I speak?"

"You may." He smiled in anticipation.

"Permission to pee, Sir?"

"No," he said slowly, as if considering the idea. "I don't think so."

"Excuse me?" She twisted back to regard him, as if she hadn't heard right.

"I said no. No, you do not have permission to pee."

Alana slowly faced forward again. She was silent, her shoulders sagging a little in her defeat. While Mark could easily go all day without peeing, Alana had a bladder the size of a walnut. Certainly, it had to be quite full at this point—he'd made sure of it.

He leaned forward and idly fondled her breasts as he gazed into the fire. How long until she asked again? Until she begged?

In less than five minutes, she tried again. "Sir? I really do need to pee. Please?"

Mark made his voice stern. "When I want to you to pee, I'll let you know. Is that understood?"

"But..." she began, but apparently thought better of it, finishing the sentence with a dutiful, "Yes, Sir."

He glanced at his watch and placed a silent bet with himself. She would last another three minutes.

She surprised him by holding on for five, but then she blurted, "Please, Sir. I really can't hold it anymore." She had begun to rock slightly backward and forward. "I'm going to have an accident."

Mark lifted his legs from her back and pretended to contemplate her plight. Then he sprang his deviously delightful plan. "I'll let you pee on one condition."

"Yes, Sir?" She looked up eagerly.

"If I let you pee, you have to let me pee first." He paused for effect before adding, "In your mouth."

Alana looked dumbstruck, as if she couldn't possibly have heard him correctly. "What?" she blurted, forgetting his honorific, but he didn't correct her.

"You heard me. In your mouth. You're serving now as my furniture. The next logical step is to use you as my toilet."

Alana had begun to shake her head, her mouth working, though she made no sound.

"Are you refusing, slave?" He allowed her the illusion for the moment that she had any choice in the matter.

Alana didn't answer, but only continued to shake her head from side to side.

Mark hadn't expected this. How dare she refuse him?

Getting to his feet, he gripped her by the shoulders and forced her to her feet. Gripping her wrists, he pulled her arms up hard behind her back and frogmarched her to the bedroom. "Your choice, Alana. I think a timeout in the cage will give you more perspective."

As he pushed her toward the closet, she finally spoke. "No, not the cage. Please, not the cage," she begged, pushing back against him.

He stopped just outside the closet doors. "So…what are you saying? Are you ready to behave? Should I forgive you for refusing your lord and Master?"

"Yes, Sir. Please, hurry."

He let go of her arms and she immediately brought her hands to her crotch, dancing on her toes like a little girl. He led her to the bathroom. When she tried to rush to the toilet, he stopped her, instead directing her to climb into the tub.

He'd been planning on making her take his urine first, but it was clear she couldn't hold it another second, so he let her pee standing up, the urine already splashing down between her shapely legs the moment she climbed in. When she reached toward the tap to wash herself, however, he stopped her.

"No, you aren't done yet. I still need to piss, too, don't forget." He pointed downward. "Get on your knees. Kneel up, arms behind your back and open your mouth."

She stared at him with horror in her wide eyes. "Please," she breathed. "I can't. Don't make me do that. Please."

He'd been more than patient, giving her more chances than she deserved, and now the bitch was refusing him yet again? Anger suddenly exploded in his brain. "How *dare* you say no to me! Not once, but twice? You've definitely earned yourself a punishment, young lady. Now, don't make it worse for yourself. Open your mouth or I'll devise a way to open it for you. And I promise it will be much worse for you if I have to do that. *Much* worse."

Alana obviously believed him. She knelt, trembling, locked her arms behind her back and opened her lips in a half-hearted gesture.

"Wider," he ordered, as he unzipped his fly and

pulled out his cock. He positioned himself over her and stood for a moment. She was shaking, her eyes squeezed shut. "Open your eyes," he commanded. "Keep them on your Master while he pisses in your mouth."

She opened her dark blue eyes and fixed them on his face, a tear rolling down her cheek.

He held his shaft in his hand and aimed for her lovely, open mouth. His cock was already hardening with arousal, so he quickly released a steady, spurting stream of urine. Some of it went into her mouth, the rest splashing in her face and hair.

The disobedient girl cried out in dismay, doubling over so that the rest of the pee hit the top of her head, drenching her hair. She was crying and gagging, clearly completely and thoroughly humiliated by the ordeal.

His anger had evaporated and Mark felt suddenly sorry for his darling girl. He tucked his cock back into his jeans and knelt beside the tub. He turned on the tap, and when the water was hot enough, he filled the pitcher he kept by the tub and poured it over the crouched girl. He wet a washcloth, rubbed it with soap, and gently washed her body. Then he plugged the tub and filled it with warm water, adding some of the bath oil she liked.

At his direction, she lay back in the tub as the water rose around her. She closed her eyes and sighed, her face still streaked with tears. All that fuss over a little piss. He would have to help her desensitize. She should welcome anything that was of him, even his piss.

Then there was the matter of her punishment. She had said no to him, not once, but repeatedly, and he couldn't let that go unpunished. But she was exhausted, and the effects of the champagne still lingered in his bloodstream. There was always tomorrow.

"Clean yourself up," he said. "Then let's go to bed. I'll punish you tomorrow."

Mark had a small workroom in the cellar. He'd just finished devising his latest toy, and he was eager to try it out. He had been intending to install the new toy up in the playroom, but had decided instead to rig it down there, for a change of venue. He'd finished out a second room with carpeting and insulated walls, and he attached a pulley mechanism in the ceiling, much like the one up in the playroom, from which he hung long, sturdy chains. In the workshop, he drilled holes in either end of a long, narrow wooden beam, and he attached the beam to the chains, creating a kind of long swing.

That day, he had Alana dress in the black satin corset he'd just ordered for her from the internet, which cinched in her already long, slender waist, accentuating her hourglass figure. Her breasts were popping over the top of the corset, revealing just a hint of nipple. She wore very high red heels that accentuated her slender ankles and long, lean calves.

He led her down the stairs and into the finished room, waving toward his new toy with a flourish. "This is called a cunt tease," he informed her proudly. "I designed it myself."

She regarded his creation with silence, her face impassive, as it usually was when he wasn't torturing or teasing her. He longed for that rare smile, but it hadn't appeared in quite a while.

He might not get a smile, but he would certainly get a reaction, once he introduced her to the formidable charms of his new toy. Leaving her to stand by the door, Mark turned the pulley mechanism until the wooden beam was lowered to calf height.

He waved her over and said, "Step over the

beam and straddle it."

Alana came forward as ordered and did as he said. She looked so hot in heels and corset, her pretty, smooth cunt and legs bare.

He raised the beam until it just touched her cunt. She looked down at it, uncertainty and the beginning of fear in her lovely face. His cock hardened in anticipation.

"Raise your arms over your head," he instructed. He attached her iron bracelets together and secured them to a chain dangling just above her. He adjusted the chain until he was satisfied that Alana could stand comfortably in her heels.

Then he began to raise the wooden beam higher, until it was wedged between her labia. "Alana," he said. "Why do you exist?"

She answered promptly, having gone through this exercise many, many times. "To serve you, Sir."

"And why else?"

"To suffer for you, Sir."

He veered slightly from the usual question and answer routine. "Do you like to suffer for me, slave?"

"If it pleases you, Sir," she said.

Would that answer ever change? Would she, someday, truly want to suffer for her Master?

He lifted the bar higher, until she was forced onto her toes, her weight was almost entirely on her splayed pussy.

"Please," she groaned. "I can't take this much longer. It really, really hurts."

"Sure you can. We're only just getting started. But here, this should distract you." He withdrew a vibrating egg from his pocket. He lowered the beam just enough so he could wedge the small toy between her sex and the beam. Pressing a switch on the remote, Mark turned on the egg, which made a humming sound as it began vibrating between the wood and her body.

He pulled out the clover clamps and approached her, yanking down the satin cups of her corset to expose her breasts. Mark pressed one clip open, and holding out her nipple, he let it close. As she gasped, he did the same with the second nipple.

Taking a step back, he used the remote to turn up the speed of the vibrating egg against her clit. He could see the sweat forming beneath her arms and along her upper lip. She began to tremble as the egg mercilessly vibrated her toward an orgasm.

"Oh, god," she moaned, the words low and sensual in her throat. In spite of the pain, or no, perhaps because of it, she was going to come. Pleasure and pain were always offered in tandem. She was rarely permitted the one without the other. She had learned to orgasm from a crop on her cunt as easily as from his tongue or deft fingers.

Mark loved to give her pleasure nearly as much as he loved to make her suffer. The combination of the two was a powerful aphrodisiac for them both. She had become a masochistic, deeply sexual being, and he knew just which buttons to push to make her come. Indeed, he'd installed some of them.

True, lust did not equal love, but for now it was enough.

Chapter 8

She had learned to handle the fear over time. To keep it at bay. To be quiet so he would relent and release her. Sometimes he rewarded her with lovely, powerful orgasms. Yes, there was pain associated with every pleasure. She understood and accepted that was how it had to be. It pleased Mark to see her suffer, and therefore it pleased her. The really weird thing was that as time had passed, the pain and pleasure sometimes fused together, blending so she couldn't tell one from the other.

At those times, she was lifted out of her body — a spirit floating just above, filled with a dark, powerful energy that was like nothing she'd ever experienced back in the before time. When she thanked her Master after those sessions, she truly meant it.

She hated to displease him, but sometimes, despite her very best efforts, she did so. Then she would try to accept her punishments with what he called submissive grace. It worked best when she could disappear into that small, secret place inside her where she no longer felt the hard wood of the paddle against her ass, or the icy water in the tub, or the brutal cut of the cane.

She could even tolerate the cage now, as long as it didn't last too long, as long as she could see that line of light beneath the closet doors. The light kept her anchored, connected to this world. When it went out, she was flung into the hard, unyielding arms of her night terrors — hours and hours alone and adrift, locked in the tight, cold confines behind metal bars, all alone.

She tried hard to be good, and so avoid the cage. It was so much nicer to sleep in her Master's warm, strong embrace. If she positioned herself just so in his bed, she nearly forgot the chains, and he was so tender with her. She didn't even mind being wakened in the night so he could use her body. After all, she belonged to him — he could do as he wished.

Alana sighed and curled a little tighter on the metal floor of the cage. She hadn't meant to displease him today — in fact, she wasn't even sure what she'd done. She rested her hands under her cheek, her eyes fixed on the line of light. He would come soon for her, she was sure of it.

She would do better, next time.

As she lay hovering on the edge of sleep, her mind drifted to the before time — before Mark. She hadn't always been here. Of course, she knew that. There was another life, another time, filled with schedules and shoots and paparazzi and parties. She'd never had a minute to breathe, to drift, as she was doing now.

She tried to capture some specific memory from the before time, but it kept slipping away, just beyond her grasp.

She sighed again. It made her head hurt to try to remember. Better to stay focused on the moment. He would come for her soon, she was sure of it. Then he might take her to the playroom for some bondage and sex play. Maybe a flogging. She loved the flogger, with its heavy, thuddy tresses of suede that stroked her skin until she was transported out of her body and went flying in that free, open space somewhere just outside of her consciousness.

Hopefully he wouldn't use the cane. She still hated the cane, even though the Master told her she should love everything that pleased him. She tried to, but it hurt so fucking much. She especially hated that sound — that terrifying whippy whistle in the instant before the rod marked her with its fiery sting.

Yet, even with the cane, she was sometimes

transported to that special place. Just when the pain became intolerable, if she was lucky, it would happen. An odd kind of serenity would fall over her like a cloak, snuffing out the fire of her panic.

Mark had explained that when that happened, she was in a state of submissive grace — of true acceptance of the gift of suffering he offered. All she knew was during those times, the orgasms she experienced were like nothing she'd even known in the before time. She had had no idea that a person could feel anything so intensely. It was like an instantly addictive drug, and she had come to crave that sensation.

As she dreamily recalled the last powerful climax, her clit gently throbbed between her legs. She imagined his tongue licking so sweetly along her labia, or the rough but welcome exploration of his fingers, or the perfect friction when he was inside her, fucking her so hard, so good…

Her hand slid down between her legs and cupped her smooth, hot cunt. *I could touch myself now. Steal an orgasm. Take a little pleasure. He would never know.*

But she didn't. It was forbidden to take her own pleasure, except under his express command. True, he couldn't see her in the dark, but why take the chance? He would know.

Somehow, Mark always knew.

She pulled her hand away and let her mind drift again, thinking back to her first days in Mark's home — *their* home, he always said, as if they were a regular couple, married even. A strange thought, but not altogether horrible…

She found she couldn't remember the first few days very well, except for the constant, pervading fear. Back then, she'd been sure he was going to kill her, but as the time passed, she understood she was safe — as long as she obeyed.

She used to think about escape, but he was clever, her Master, and whenever he left her alone, which wasn't often, he made sure to keep her shackled and restrained. There was no escape. This was her life now.

He was her life now.

She should hate him.

She did hate him, didn't she?

Yes.

But also…no.

She certainly needed him, depended on him for her very survival. She thought of him constantly, as her world was now focused exclusively on her

Master. What would he do today? Would he be in a kind mood or a grumpy one? Would he use the cane today, or the flogger? Would he make tender love to her in the bed, or would he grab her from behind while she was washing dishes, throw her to the floor and take her with violence from behind, his hand clamped hard over her mouth?

Would he be pleased with her? Would he find her submissive enough? Beautiful enough? Responsive enough?

She used to despise him. She did remember that. Even while she was pretending to submit and to obey, inside she had seethed with rage, but that feeling — all that anger — it had taken so much energy to hold onto. And for what? It only left her miserable and frightened.

But when had the change come? When had the pretending transformed into a real desire to please, to serve, to submit? It had happened slowly, like water dripping onto stone, slowly reshaping it into something new.

But did she love him?

No.

Because love had to be a choice, and she had none.

Yet, she had no doubt he loved her—he truly did.

It seemed impossible, and no one outside their secluded existence would ever be able to understand, but she knew in her bones that Mark loved her as no one ever had—utterly and completely. His every act toward her, however degrading or harsh it might seem to an outsider, was suffused with love.

Yet, how did one reconcile the love with the cruelty? How could the things he did to her—the whippings, the caning, the forced sex, the humiliation—be acts of love?

It was all so confusing. Better not to think so much. What was the point? Things were as they were. She belonged to Mark. Mark was her world. He would die for her—she was sure of it.

If he didn't end up killing her first.

~*~

Alana lay on her back on the kitchen table. Her legs hung over the edge of the table, tightly secured to the table legs. Her thighs were spread wide, her ass right at the spot where a dinner plate might sit, her lovely cunt spread wide. Her arms were stretched over her head, and tied securely at the wrists with strong nylon rope.

Mark loved the way the rope looked knotted around her body. The hard, dark wood of the table contrasted nicely with her soft, pale skin. He had rouged her nipples and her mouth with red to heighten the contrast, and the black silk blindfold was the perfect touch.

They had finished dinner, and Alana was dessert. Mark stripped off his clothes and sat in front of his slave girl. He lowered his face to her smooth mons and rested his cheek lightly against her. After a moment, he lifted his head, this time lowering it until his lips touched the petals of her cunt. Slowly, lovingly, he tasted, licked and teased her sex.

It wasn't long before Alana began to moan, her pelvis lifting toward his mouth.

Mark laughed and playfully swatted her sex with his hand. "Slut," he whispered, but he was pleased. He inserted a finger deep into her cunt. She was wet and tight.

Moving his finger inside her, he asked, "Are you ready for fun?"

Alana licked her lips. "Yes, Sir."

Mark slapped her pussy sharply with his palm.

She gasped and jerked in her restraints, unprepared.

Her breathy cry thrilled him, so he hit her again, and again. When her cunt was red from the impromptu beating, Mark again dipped his head, kissing and suckling the swelling, heated flesh.

Again, within a minute or so, she was moaning and arching toward him as best as she could, given the rope restraints. He licked and teased her clit, a finger moving in the tight heat inside her.

Just as she approached climax, he stopped.

A small sigh of frustration escaped that perfect mouth. "Don't stop," she begged. Then she gasped, clearly aware of her transgression, though of course it was too late to take it back.

Nor would he let her get away with it. "How *dare* you tell me what to do?" Mark demanded, though he loved what a total slut she had become. "Have you forgotten all your training? You obviously need a stern, painful reminder."

Alana began to whimper quietly. She knew better than ask what her punishment would be.

Mark selected a long red candle he had ready for this occasion. His hand shook with excitement as he lit the candle, causing a drop of melted wax to fall on his own finger. It was hot — perfect.

Holding the candle over her stomach, he let the first series of scalding drops fall.

Alana cried out, no doubt startled by the sudden, unexpected splatter of heat. She continued to jerk a little as he moved the candle slowly up her torso, leaving a line of red dots along the skin.

He circled a nipple with red droplets. Alana yelped when the hot wax landed directly on her nipple.

Barely able to contain his excitement, Mark circled the second nipple with melted wax and aimed a scalding drop on her tender nubbin.

His cock was hard as a rock. He blew out the candle and pushed it carefully into her spread pussy. She grunted a little, but knew better than to try and push it out. He stepped back to admire her sluttish look as he fisted his cock, which was aching for attention.

He pulled out a chair and climbed onto the table. Straddling Alana's chest, he leaned forward and lightly smacked at her lips with the head of his cock. The obedient slut at once opened her pretty mouth, and he leaned forward, moving his shaft until the tip lodged at the back of her throat.

He thrust back and forth, groaning with pleasure as she did her best to worship her Master's cock in her awkward position. He didn't want to come though, not yet. Alana hadn't yet suffered enough. Pulling away from her eager bird's mouth, he climbed off the girl and retrieved the candle, now redolent with the heady scent of her juices.

He lit it again and held the flame just above her spread pussy. The wax began to drip in a steady, scalding stream over the delicate folds.

"Ah," Alana cried, the pain ripe in her throaty voice. "Please, Sir. It hurts, it hurts!"

"It's supposed to," Mark said with a laugh. He let the hot liquid fall until her cunt was coated in a red cap of drying wax.

Satisfied, he again straddled his girl and shoved his cock down her throat. He pumped fast and hard, making her gag, which only spurred him on. Within seconds he shot his prolific load down her throat.

When he could catch his breath, he climbed off the table. Though he wasn't yet ready to remove her restraints, he did take off her blindfold. He wanted her to watch what came next.

Reaching for the single tail, he snapped it in the air near her body. She bit her lower lip in that sweet way she had when she was nervous, but otherwise betrayed no reaction.

"I'll need to remove the wax from your pretty cunt," he said with a cruel smile. He flicked the leather tail, the tip catching the edge of the wax cap.

She cried out her pain.

"Take it," he advised her. "You earned it."

With carefully aimed strokes, he flicked away the hardened wax, and when he was done, all that was left was her sweet cunt, red and welted, and perfect for fucking. She was crying quietly.

Dropping the whip, he took his pleasure.

Snow was falling thick and fast outside. Inside it was cozy and warm. Alana shifted, swaying gently in the thick leather cuffs lined with sheepskin that held her upside down in the dungeon, her long hair brushing the white floor. Her arms were tightly secured around her back, the iron bracelets clipped together.

Mark leaned down and held the single tail lash

he called the stinger to her lips, and she dutifully kissed the handle.

"Are you ready to suffer for me, cunt?"

"Yes, Sir," Alana whispered, because that was the only answer permitted. Yet, despite her fear, perhaps partially because of it, her nipples stiffened and there was a clutch of desire in her sex as he moved closer.

Mark caressed her thighs with his hands. He kissed her inner thighs, his touch as light as a butterfly's wing. She shivered as his mouth moved closer toward her spread sex. She felt his warm breath against her pussy. She sighed as his velvet tongue began to glide slowly between her folds, and abandoned herself to the exquisite pleasure.

Then came the sudden, sharp sting of the lash on her inner thigh. Alana screamed, caught completely unaware, though she shouldn't have been. Hadn't she learned all too well that with the pleasure must come the pain?

She retreated into herself as the lash rained across her flesh, the pain coiling like fire in her nerve endings. Finally, the whipping stopped. She was too dizzy and disoriented to even try to lift her head as she heard Mark move away. She just swayed, eyes closed, waiting for whatever came next.

When he returned, she felt the insistent nudge of something at her cunt. As it slid inside her, she felt the familiar, hard fullness of a vibrator, and she grunted as he pressed it deeper. He flicked a switch at the base and it whirred into life.

It pulsated and tickled inside of Alana's pussy, vibrating her clit, instantly arousing her. Though these battery-induced orgasms were never as satisfying as his fingers, his mouth, his cock, nevertheless, they were relentless in their vibrating persistence, and it wasn't long before she hovered on the edge of a climax.

"Please, Sir, may I—" she began breathlessly, but before she could complete the question, the vibrator was pulled from her body.

"No. Not yet."

She forgot her frustration as the Master brought the cruel whip down on her bare, exposed sex. As it made searing contact with her clit, Alana screamed and begged for mercy. But there was none.

He whipped her cunt with ruthless strokes, and she couldn't do a thing to stop him, held wide open by the leather and chains that suspended her. Pain exploded through her nerve endings, overloading her with sensation. She squeezed her eyes shut beneath the silk blindfold, whimpering and moaning as she struggled to take what he gave her, but it was too much — too much.

"I can't, I can't, I can't," she heard someone moaning, the sound distant to her own ears. The words faded away, replaced by a steady, rising ringing. Then the inky blackness came to claim her. With a relieved sigh, she stepped into its arms.

~*~

Mark dropped the lash and quickly lowered Alana to the floor. He released the chains from the cuffs and leaned over her, pulling the blindfold from her eyes.

"Alana?"

Remorse assailed him as he gazed at her swollen, red cunt. The trickle of blood at once repelled and excited him, and his cock was stiff with need.

He lightly slapped her face. "Alana, wake up. Open your eyes."

Her lids fluttered open and she fixed him with a dilated, unfocused gaze. "Wha…?" she said, confusion etching her features.

"You passed out. That's unacceptable," Mark admonished. "It's a way of running from me."

"I'm sorry, Sir," she mumbled, her words slurred. "I didn't mean to run from you."

He looked at her carefully. Was she merely parroting what she thought he wanted to hear?

He stroked her cheek and she turned her head to kiss his hand. He pulled it away, startled by this subservient, almost loving gesture.

The thick fringe of her lashes brushed her soft cheeks, and a single tear rolled down her cheek.

"Why are you crying?"

A silly question, as her poor cunt had to be on fire. But to his surprise, she said, "I've displeased you, Sir." Another tear fell.

Shocked, Mark didn't know what to say. He tilted her chin up and lightly kissed her soft lips. Was she sincere? That kiss, like a dog licking its master's hand. And that tear — was it truly because she felt remorse and sorrow for having displeased him?

Something was different, that was for sure, though he didn't yet understand completely what it was. Her behavior no longer seemed solely motivated by fear or avoidance of pain. Something else was happening between them. Something he felt but wasn't ready to thoroughly examine.

It might disappear if he approached it, dissipating like a wisp of smoke if he got too close.

As the days passed, Alana continued in this newfound apparent devotion. Mark wanted to be happy — wasn't this what he'd always dreamed of, from the moment he first hatched his plans? The transformation seemed genuine. She had become his dream girl — compliant, obedient, highly sexed and utterly focused on him. Could these things in their sum approximate love?

There was one area, however, where his slave lacked grace. She was still afraid of the cane. He had but to mention its use and her eyes would widen with fear, her breath coming in ragged gasps as she tried to control her reaction.

As they lay in bed, Mark glanced down at the sleeping woman in his arms. His cock nudged against her warm body as he contemplated marking her ass with the new fiberglass cane he'd purchased online. At only an eighth of an inch thick, he knew it would provide a harsh sting. The business end was made of smooth white fiberglass.

The handle was ribbed with rubber for a good grip. It was the middle of the night, but he couldn't sleep, so why should she?

"Wake up," he said into Alana's hair.

Her eyes opened as she struggled to focus.

"I can't sleep," he informed her. "I'm going to cane you to relax."

Her eyes widened, her hands flying to her mouth. "Not the cane!" she blurted. She bit her lip. That protest alone was enough for punishment, but he let it pass as he unlocked the chains that held her iron bracelets. He pushed her from the bed, pressing her shoulder so she knelt on the floor as he climbed out of the bed.

"Crawl to the playroom and wait for me."

"May I use the toilet first, Sir?"

"No."

He detected the slightest hint of a sigh, but after a moment, she dropped dutifully to her hands and knees and crawled out of the bedroom, her gorgeous ass swaying.

When he came into the playroom Alana was kneeling up, her back straight as she sat back on her haunches, her legs spread as he had taught her.

When he showed her the blindfold, she lifted her chin and closed her eyes, waiting with absolute serenity.

She was breathtaking.

I love you.

He placed the blindfold over her eyes. "Stand up," he ordered and she obeyed. He raised her arms and she held them aloft, wrists touching. He clipped a chain to her cuffs, and then to the metal bar hanging from the ceiling. He admired her naked body for a moment, the long, slender waist, the high, full breasts, the gently flaring hips. He reached down and cupped her pussy, inserting a finger deep into her cunt. She was wet, wonderfully wet, but he could see the fear in her eyes. What a perfect combination.

Mark held the new fiberglass cane to her lips. She kissed it. He placed the tip against her lips. They parted. He inserted the cane several inches into her mouth and pressed down, forcing her to open her mouth wide. She began to tremble.

Withdrawing the cane, he walked around behind her. Slowly he dragged the rod across her back, down to her ass. She remained still, but the pace of her breathing had picked up. Mark returned to stand in front of her. He leaned close so their naked bodies were touching. He brought his arms around her, holding the cane in both hands, imprisoning her between his body and the cane.

He could feel her heart pounding against him. He could see she was afraid. And brave. And willing. He stepped back from her and again walked behind the bound woman. He spit on the cane's handle and rubbed the saliva over it as a lubricant.

Alana let out a sudden cry as he inserted the rubber handle of the cane into her ass.

He took a step back. What a picture she made, hung and naked, with the cane hanging lewdly from her ass. Mark held it there a moment longer, testing her grace, testing her resistance.

"Whose ass is that, slave?"

"Yours, Sir," she managed between clenched teeth.

"That's right, my love. It's mine. If I wanted to, I could have you bare your asshole so I could cane it until it bled. Isn't that right?"

"Yes, Sir," she said in a tiny, frightened voice. He could smell her fear. And her desire. Mark withdrew the rod from her luscious bottom. The time had come. Let the dance begin.

The first blow landed suddenly, across the front of her thighs. She hissed her pain. Again the cane struck, this time behind her, on her ass, across both cheeks. Aiming a few inches lower, he let the cane strike her flesh again. The welts were beautiful. The only sound in the room was the whistle of the cane, the crack on her flesh, and her breathing, ragged and rasping in her throat.

When the cane landed across her breasts Alana wailed, losing control of her bladder. Urine trickled down her legs as she danced and hopped in her efforts to avoid the cruel bite of the rod. Aware of what she'd done, she blushed a dark, brick red. She would suffer for her lack of control, and they both knew it.

He brought the cane to her lips again. After a moment, she kissed it. Then he smacked her breasts again, bringing the cane down hard on her tender flesh. Alana screamed. He knew, because of the kiss she had thought they were done, but they were only just beginning.

~*~

Alana's arms were numb. Her body was covered in lines of fire, sweat stinging the welts. Her blindfold was damp with tears. She could sense Mark close by, and knew by the slippery slap of his hand against his spit-lubricated cock that he was masturbating.

Every ounce of strength had been caned from her and she sagged against her restraints, relieved it was over. She was desperately thirsty, but lacked the strength even to form the words, to push forth the breath it would require to ask for a drink of water.

Mark was breathing heavily near her. He moved in closer, moaning as he ejaculated across her belly and pussy. Why hadn't he fucked her, as he usually did after a caning? Then she remembered her loss of control, and heat rose again in her cheeks as she moved her feet to avoid the puddle of urine between them. Of course he wouldn't want to fuck her in her disgrace, and who could blame him?

If only he would let her down. She wanted to be taken into his arms and soothed. She longed to feel his warm, soft lips pressed against hers. She needed him to wash her, to groom her, to wipe away the sweat, the piss and the pain.

Then he might make love to her. Tender, aching, passionate love.

For a moment, a conflicting thought pushed its way, unwelcome, into her mind. What the fuck was wrong with her? This man was her tormentor, her captor, and she wanted him to touch her, to hold her, to make love to her? She should be screaming her outrage. She should be finding a way to escape…

No. Hush. There's no escape. Shh, let it go. Easier to obey, to submit, to surrender…

She felt the chains loosening, falling away. Mark caught her and lifted her tenderly into his strong, sure embrace. He carried her to the bathroom and laid her gently on the thick bath mat near the tub. He hadn't removed the blindfold, but she could hear the running water, then feel the warm touch of a wet washcloth gently washing her legs and sore pussy.

Then a soft towel was gently patted over her bruised flesh, and finally she felt the soothing salve spread over her skin and lightly smoothed over her labia. Each touch of his fingers hurt her, but also soothed her. She didn't protest or even move.

Then his arms slid beneath her body, and she was again lifted and carried back into the bedroom, where he lay her gently on the bed. When he removed the blindfold, she saw that the room was lit by the pink and gold light of a new dawn.

He leaned over her and lightly kissed her dry, cracked lips. "I'll be right back," he said.

She lay still while he was gone, too exhausted to

move.

He returned with a bottle of cold water. He
unscrewed the cap and held it to Alana's lips,
cradling her head as she drank. When the bottle
was empty, he let her head fall back onto the
pillows.

When she awoke some time later, Mark was
asleep beside her, his arm thrown across her body
like a shield, like a chain.

Lately, Mark liked for Alana to cook breakfast,
and she enjoyed the simple, domestic task. She
placed the plate of pancakes on the table beside the
bacon and took her place on her cushion by her
Master's chair.

As Mark shared his food with her, he said, "I'm
thinking of piercing your cunt so you can wear my
jewelry."

Alana's stomach did a sudden, unpleasant lurch.
The idea of a needle piercing her flesh was
terrifying. Yet at the same time…

"What do you think?" he asked, his eyes intent
on her face.

What did she think?

She blinked in her confusion. She was not used
to being asked her thoughts on anything of this

import. Was the question rhetorical, or did he really require a response?

He seemed to be waiting for an answer. Was it a trick question?

Not sure herself of her feelings, Alana replied, "I'm afraid of needles, Sir."

"I understand. But the question I'm asking is, would you like to wear my jewelry at your cunt, slave girl? Would it please you to please me in that way?"

Ah. Now he had phrased it in a way she could understand. "Yes, Sir."

"Excellent. We'll do it tonight."

Chapter 9

Mark held out a glass. "Drink this. It's brandy to help dull the pain a bit."

Alana accepted the glass and drained it, enjoying the sweet burn as it went down.

Mark took the glass from her and set it aside. "I'm going to tie you down to keep you still. We wouldn't want any sudden movement while I'm using the needle."

She lay on the bed, and he placed pillows under her ass to raise her hips. He had her bend her knees, feet flat on the mattress. Using soft ties, he looped one around each thigh and tied them tightly to the posts of the bed, securing her open and spread for him. Next, he bound her wrists, pulling the ties tight.

In spite of her determination to submit with grace, Alana's heart had begun to pound, and her mouth was dry with fear.

Mark leaned over a tray on the nightstand and held up a smooth oval hoop of gold, about three inches long and a quarter inch thick. It was beautiful, and for a moment, Alana nearly forgot her fear.

"It's lovely, isn't it?" Mark said with a smile. He touched the open clasp, not unlike the hook of an earring. "When I release the pin, it will spring permanently shut, a constant symbol of ownership."

He set down the jewelry and took a piece of ice from a small metal bowl. He held the ice to her labia until they were frozen and numb.

Alana shivered.

He picked up the threading needle he would use to pierce her flesh.

Alana closed her eyes.

"Okay, Alana," he said, leaning over her. "Stay very still. Understand?"

"Yes, Sir," she whispered, her breath catching in her throat.

She felt the tension at her sex as he pulled the flesh taut.

"Okay, take a deep breath and count to three.

Then let it out."

She did so, relaxing slightly as she exhaled.

"Again."

This time, as she exhaled on the third count, she felt a stinging pinch, and she jerked in her bonds, crying out a little.

"Shh, it's done. You did very well. I just need to thread the jewelry through now. Stay still."

Alana tried to stop trembling as he finished his work. It really hadn't been bad at all. Nevertheless, she was glad she was lying down, because the world was spinning beneath her eyelids. Then she felt his lips lightly touching hers.

"It's done, baby," he crooned. "You were very brave. And it's beautiful."

Alana opened her eyes and smiled. There was a dull throb of pain where the needle had pierced her, but nothing she couldn't tolerate. She could feel the weight of the gold now locked into her flesh. She lay still as Mark untied her restraints and gently removed the pillows from under her body.

"May I see it?" she asked, not quite believing the whole thing was over.

Mark brought a small hand mirror and helped

her to sit up. The gold hoop lay against her thigh, its clasp glinting at her labium. Alana stared at the jewelry and then up at Mark.

He was watching her intently, something like pain moving over his features.

"I love you," he said, his voice cracking with emotion.

Alana's mouth fell open. He had never said those three words before, though he'd danced around them many times. This was the man who owned her, who controlled her, who used her, who was obsessed with her — and those concepts she understood.

Months of training, deprivation and constant sexual stimulation with no distractions from the outside world had fixated Alana's focus completely on the man standing before her, the man who had just said out loud at last that he loved her.

She knew he wanted her to say it back. She thought perhaps she would. She would test the words in the air. See how it felt. She knew it would please him. And when Mark was pleased, things went better for his slave girl. She pursed her lips as if to speak, but somehow the words caught in her throat. She couldn't will them to form on her tongue.

"Thank you, Sir," she managed instead.

~*~

Alana's piercing healed well. Mark had been careful not to whip or fuck her cunt until it was fully healed, with no sign of infection or problem. While he was waiting, he used her ass instead.

He loved to force her down to her knees and have her spread her own cheeks and huskily beg for him to fuck her in the ass, the gold slave jewelry swaying between her thighs.

Alana would moan, and sometimes cry out if he was rough, but she never asked for mercy. She never tried to pull away. She would thank him for using her, and kiss his feet when he was done.

This morning he had pronounced her ready to resume all her proper duties as his sex slave. Now Alana stood in the playroom, wearing only spiked high heels and nipple clamps, along with the slave jewelry at her wrists and cunt.

Mark approached her with a long gold chain in his hand, a scene from one of his favorite books, *Story of O*, in his mind. "This is your leash, my pet. But instead of attaching it to a collar, I'm going to attach it to your pretty little pussy."

Gently, he took hold of the gold hoop between

her legs, and attached the leash to it. He pulled on it slightly as he walked around the room, forcing his slave to keep up. Her heels click-clacked on the wooden floor as he led her around in a large circle.

"Perhaps I should take my pet for a walk outside?"

Mark smiled with anticipation as he led Alana from the playroom, leading her by her cunt. He took a long coat from the closet and put it on the naked woman. Removing her high heels, he replaced them with the rain boots. Then he led her out into the snow.

He hadn't zipped the coat, and he noted with approval that Alana didn't do so herself. The day was sunny and windless, though it couldn't have been more than thirty degrees. After a minute or so, Alana began to shiver as he led her around and around the yard, pulling at her cunt every few paces to force her to keep up with him. She slipped once and almost fell, but managed to regain her balance.

After the walk, he led her back into the warm kitchen. He took off her coat and the leash, and had her kneel in her usual spot beside his chair. He served her hot cocoa, then directed her to position herself on the table in front of him, her legs spread wide.

He fingered her pussy, pleased as her nipples stiffened and her cunt grew moist and swollen at his touch. "Who do you belong to, cunt girl?"

"You, Sir."

"What will you do for me?"

"Whatever you wish, Sir."

Was that really true? How far would she go? How far did he dare to take her? Did she really belong to him now? If he took off her manacles and chains and unlocked all the doors, would she remain? Would she still claim she was his? Would she still be willing to suffer for him?

When he had finally, finally said those three simple words — *I love you* — she had not responded in kind. He could demand obedience and grace. He could make her suffer and he could give her pleasure, but he couldn't make her love him.

He stood from the table and stared down at the woman he'd stolen from the world. No, he couldn't demand her heart, but he could claim her body and her soul.

~*~

Alana was tied to a chair in the center of the playroom. Her eyes were covered in a long red satin blindfold that wound around her head to cover her mouth as well. Her ears were plugged, all sound muffled and distant. Loops of fine black nylon rope were coiled around her body, crisscrossing tightly across her flesh. Her legs were spread open, rope looped from thigh to ankle.

She couldn't move, speak, see or hear. But she could feel. She felt Mark's large strong hands smoothing their way across her bound breasts, pausing to tweak and twist the nipples that poked out between the ropes. She felt the hands slide down her stomach and between her legs. He tugged gently on the gold hoop nestled against her pussy.

His fingers danced around her clit, which throbbed with anticipation of his touch. He stroked her until she moaned against her gag, but then the hand was withdrawn, and a moment later she felt the leathery sting of a riding crop on her inner thigh. He smacked her methodically, covering every square inch of her thighs until they were on fire, and she was whimpering steadily into the satin gag.

Just when she couldn't endure another stroke of the crop, it stopped. After a moment, Mark's heavy weight was suddenly straddling her legs. He maneuvered himself so his cock was level with her spread cunt, and with one smooth thrust, he pressed himself into her. He filled her completely as he began to rock inside of her. She was pressed back hard against the unyielding wood of the chair.

The sensation of being fucked while tightly bound, with both sight and sound cut off, was overwhelming. She might have been a statue, carved of stone, unable to respond, save for the pounding of her heart and the throb in her cunt.

He came quickly, and pulled away, his heavy weight suddenly gone, a trickle of semen left on her thigh.

She waited for him to release the knots of rope at her wrists and ankles, to unwind the tight bindings that made her breasts ache. She waited for him to unwind the silk wrapped around her face, and to remove the plugs still blocking her ears. She waited, straining to hear his movements, to guess what he might be doing.

Finally she understood she was alone.

He had left her there.

She dozed lightly, floating to a dreamy space where there was no pain. Revisiting her recurring dream, she saw the lovely slave girls dancing on the soft harem rugs for their sultan king. The women were young, barely more than girls, with dewy skin the color of pecan shells. Their almond shaped eyes were lined in kohl, their mouths glistening like red fruit. They wore the same jewelry as Alana, iron bracelets at their wrists and ankles, gold hoops glinting between their legs.

The young dancers dipped and rose, as graceful as gazelles, making a slow circle around the solitary man. She tried to see his face, but it was in shadow, hidden in a swirling mist. Who was the man? Was it Mark? She didn't know. She leaned forward, straining to discover the secret Master of her secret dreams. The room was clearing, the mist burning away. In a moment she would see his face…

Suddenly Alana snapped back to reality as she became aware of Mark's presence. She could hear him moving about in the room. She licked her lips beneath the gag, which had loosened. They were dry. Her mouth felt like cotton.

There was fumbling at the back of her head. Then the gag was pulled from her mouth, though not her eyes. Then a straw was poking against her chapped lips. Alana eagerly drank the cool water, grateful for its sweetness on her parched tongue.

She shifted in her bonds, eager for him to remove them. But there was only the sound of receding footsteps, then the soft click of the closing door.

Tears pricked at her eyelids, but she willed herself not to panic. He would be back in a second. Soon, any moment now, he'd come back, untie the rope and lift her into his tender embrace.

Alana tried to drift back to the harem dream, but it would not return to her. She was alone in the white, bare room, with dried semen itching on her leg and pussy, her skin still sore and stinging from the crop. On top of her discomfort, she needed to pee, as usual. If only she could close her legs. If only he would hurry back to release her.

She drifted again into a fretful doze. These dreams were darker. A sinister, evil man was chasing her down long, dark alleys. Though she had to escape him, she desperately had to pee. She had just crouched behind a dumpster to relieve herself when she was startled awake.

She hadn't heard him enter, but again a drinking straw was being poked between her lips. She didn't dare take another drink. She didn't want to pee on herself, and the pressure in her bladder was intense. Keeping her lips pressed together, she shook her head slightly and turned away.

Mark pulled the plugs from her ears. "Drink," he said.

It wasn't a request.

Alana sipped at the straw, drawing in as little liquid as possible.

"Are you ready to be untied?"

"Yes, please, Sir."

He removed the blindfold, and she blinked as her eyes adjusted to the light. He crouched in front of her to untie the knots and unwind the rope from her body. Her flesh was indented and red where the ropes had been, and her limbs tingled painfully as blood flow returned.

Mark slipped off her heels and helped her to a shaky stand. "Let's get you cleaned up. Then, if you ask very nicely, I might let you pee."

Sadistic fucking bastard!

The words had slipped unbidden into her mind and she tried to push them away. Absurd to waste energy being angry at Mark. He was unassailable. There was no point to resist. Better to flow, to accept, to obey. She let the errant flash of anger disappear like a pebble sinking beneath the water, out of reach, away from conscious thought.

She lay in the bed on fresh sheets, her Master crouched between her legs. Leaning up, he licked and suckled her nipples until she moaned. His tongue trailed down her body, stopping between her legs.

Alana sighed her pleasure as his mouth found her sweet spot. It felt good…so good…

He tongued her clit as he slid a hard finger inside her, sending shocks of pleasure and heat through her body. As the tide of an orgasm rose, she gasped, "Please, oh! Mark, Sir, may I—"

Her request was aborted by his fingers moving inside her like a cock, thrusting with perfect timing and friction as he sucked on her hard clit. She knew she had to try, and from somewhere inside she found the breath to say, "…come?"

He might have said yes, she wasn't sure, but she could no longer control herself as she spilled over the edge of consciousness into blinding ecstasy. Mark continued to kiss her, fucking her with his fingers as she spasmed helplessly against him. She would pay—she knew she would have to pay, but for now, she floated in the bliss…

~*~

Alana lay sprawled, legs akimbo, pussy open like a sticky, wilted orchid. Her eyes had fluttered shut and her breathing had slowed. Mark gazed at her lovely naked body, her full, luscious lips, her dark lashes shadowing her cheeks.

She had responded with such intensity, such abandonment, to his kisses. Sometimes she seemed almost happy to be with him, but was it simply a way to adapt? She was his prisoner, with absolutely no choice in the matter.

He had demanded submission, and she had succumbed. He had taught her well, and she obeyed him in almost everything now, as quickly and demurely as possible.

When she did disobey or fail to please him, he punished her soundly. She knew she deserved it. She never complained or begged to be set free, like she had in the beginning.

Things were good, right? As good as they could be, given that he'd taken what wasn't his and twisted it to meet his needs.

Mark sighed heavily and looked away from the sleeping girl. What more did he want? How far did he have to go until he would feel safe? For that was really it, wasn't it? He would never feel safe, because she could never prove her love for him with her servitude. Precisely because it was forced. Precisely because he had taken her against her will. It wasn't a love freely given. It didn't belong to him.

He had stolen it.

The idea had slowly been forming for some time now. He had done extensive research into the process. He had come up with a design. He had begun to practice on raw chicken breasts.

He had thought of doing something with his initials, but that had seemed too obvious. The design was simple. It was based on the two oval links that held Alana's wrist and ankle bracelets together. He had purchased eighteen-gauge galvanized sheet metal, which he had cut with tin snips. He had made several models, trying to get it just right. He practiced using a pair of large insulated pliers to hold the molded tin in the propane torch. It took a while to get the metal heated to just the right temperature.

The tin design had turned red-hot for a moment, then faded back to its original silver, keeping its shape beautifully. He had pressed the hot metal against the chicken flesh again and again, until he'd created a perfect brand.

At last he was ready to try it on the real thing.

~*~

That evening after dinner, Mark said, "Alana, what are you?"

Alana looked up. She had been staring into the fire, daydreaming at his feet. "Your slave, Sir," she answered automatically.

"What are you willing to do for me?"

"Whatever you command of me, Sir." Her stomach did a small loop-de-loop. Something was coming—probably not something good. She tried not to tense. Not to anticipate.

"If I wish to beat you," he said calmly, "you would allow me to?"

"Of course, Sir."

What did he mean, would she *allow* it? How could she stop it?

She glanced up at his face again. He was looking, not at her, but into the dancing, crackling flames before them. "And if I wished to cane you, would you allow it?"

"Yes, Sir." She couldn't control the slight tremor the mention of a caning caused her. *Please, not the cane.*

"And if I wished to pierce your flesh with my needle?"

"But you already—"

"Answer the question. I'm speaking hypothetically."

"Yes, Sir."

"And if I choose to bind you in rope, fill you with dildos, lock you in your cage, deny you food or drink, would you allow this?"

"It's your prerogative, Sir. I belong to you."

"Yes. You do." He paused, then continued, "I've been thinking, Alana. You exhibit all the signs of a submissive slave. But we both know you didn't come here of your own volition. Nor do I choose to set you free. You belong to me. Your body belongs to me."

She sensed he was about to get to his real purpose. She watched his face, anxious now, waiting.

He looked at last from the fire directly at her. "I have decided I want to mark you — permanently."

A tattoo, she thought with some relief. *That would be all right.*

There was something fierce in his expression. Something determined. His eyes dropped, roaming her body. "Do you understand, slave?"

"I think so, Sir. Did you mean a tattoo?"

"No. I mean this." He took the bag from the end table by the couch and carefully removed a piece of what looked like tin with a raised design stamped into it.

Alana stared at it, confused.

"This is a brand, Alana. I want to brand you. It would be a beautiful symbol of our perfect union." His gaze was a flame running up and down her body. Heat flowed up to her cheeks. His words burned behind her eyes.

She opened her mouth to respond, but found she didn't know what to say. Her first instinct was to shout, *no*! But something stayed her tongue. That word had almost dropped from her vocabulary, from her way of thinking. It wasn't an option even to be considered. She stared, fascinated at the pretty design of the interlinked ovals.

Mark watched her, his eyes flickering over her face as if he were memorizing the lines. Then he pulled her up to him. Gently he pressed her over his knee. Was he going to spank her?

But no—he touched her ass with the metal piece he held in his hand. Alana stilled like a trapped animal. The tin was cold on her flesh, but her mind was on fire. A brand. He was going to burn that design into her flesh. Could she bear it? Would she resist him? But what good would it do? If he were determined, he would simply use force—pin her down, bind her into position, and do as he wished.

Mark set the brand aside and gently stroked her ass. Speaking softly, he said, "I want your permission, slave girl. I want you to want this too. I don't want to force it on you. I want you to offer it."

He slipped his hand between her legs and began to rub her clit, swirling his finger in circles around it, then sliding the finger deep into the smooth, tight heat of her cunt.

"Offer it to me, slave. Offer me your flesh." His

voice was low, mesmerizing. Alana shifted and moaned, loving the feel of his fingers against her, in her.

In her mind's eye she saw the pretty image of the looped rings and suddenly realized what they were—the clasps to her ankle and wrists bracelets—bracelets that had never been removed since he had placed them there that first day.

The image blurred as his fingers danced upon her, suffusing her body and mind with intense pleasure. Just as she arched up to meet those fingers, to ask for release, he said again, "Offer it to me, Alana. Give me what is mine."

His words distracted her from the oncoming orgasm. Why was he asking her? Why was he forcing her to make this decision? It would be better just to do it! How cruel to force her involvement on this level—to make her commit herself to this disfigurement.

She moaned as he stroked her cunt. She needed to come. He would take what he wanted, no matter what she said. Better to say yes, to give him what was already his.

"Yes," she whispered, "Take it. Take what is yours, Sir."

~*~

It was dark out. Somehow nighttime seemed the most appropriate time for this symbolic, almost sacred act. Alana lay face down on a quilt on the kitchen table. To help her keep still, he had tied her wrists and ankles to the legs of the table with long red silk sashes.

He loved the contrast of the crimson against her pale skin. Her back, ass and thighs were crosshatched with fading lash marks and welts, overlain with newer ones. The marks were a lovely tribute — concrete evidence of her willingness to suffer for him.

And now he would give her the ultimate mark. A brand. A burning into her flesh of the symbol he had chosen for her.

If only he could brand love into her heart.

He shoved that stupid thought away. He had everything he could expect, and it was enough. It had to be.

He went through the steps again in his head. The key was to make sure the brand was hot enough. You had to press down firmly, but not too hard. He wanted the scarring deep, but not so deep that the design would be obscured. It had to be perfect. Alana deserved perfection.

She lay quietly, her cheek resting against the soft quilt. He could sense her fear, but also her control. As when he'd pierced her, he had given her a large glass of brandy, which had helped to relax her.

Mark set the propane torch into the stand he had devised, angling it until he was satisfied. Taking the small sack that held the brand design, he opened it and carefully removed the tin design.

Bending over her, Mark kissed Alana's head. "Are you ready, slave girl?"

She swallowed visibly, but then nodded. "Yes, Sir," she whispered.

Taking the large pair of disinfected, insulated pliers, he placed the design into it, closing it so that the grips held it firmly in place. He flicked the propane torch, causing it to burst into a long, hot blue flame.

Alana gasped and stared into the flame. She had an expression not unlike an animal trapped in the headlights. But that animal could run. Alana wasn't going anywhere.

Mark was intent on his task, barely focused on the terror in his slave's eyes. Not that that would have stopped him. He was fully concentrated on what he was doing as he held the metal design in the flame, watching it heat to just the proper point for the strike.

Quickly, before it cooled, he brought the metal to her soft flesh. He held it there for several seconds. The sharp smell of burning flesh filled the air.

Alana screamed.

He lifted the brand.

The deed was done.

Chapter 10

Mark was careful with his slave girl after her branding. The strike had been perfect, and though scabs would form over the wound, when they fell off, he was sure the brand would be true to its design. After a few days, he would remove the sterile dressing so the wound could breathe as it finished healing.

Because he didn't want to risk disturbing the healing process, he restrained himself from their daily whipping and fucking, though that didn't stop him from using her lovely mouth.

He had noticed that she grimaced sometimes when he ejaculated on her tongue, as if she didn't like his taste. He decided to call her on it. "You don't seem to really enjoy swallowing my jism. What's that about? You should love it, because it belongs to your Master."

"Oh, no, Sir," Alana began, though her eyes darted away from him as they did when she was lying.

He cut her off. "Don't deny it. You take it, sure. You have to. But you don't seem to love it, to crave it, the way a real slut should. Am I right about that? And think before you answer, because if you hold back any bit of the truth, I'll just beat it out of you eventually. You know I demand complete honesty from my slave."

Alana again started to protest, but as his words apparently sank in, she quieted. "Please, Sir," she began, "It's not that I don't like it. I'm — I'm just not very good at it."

He lifted his eyebrows, but pretended to accept the half-truth. "Well then," he said with a sudden, cruel grin. "I'll just have to help you get better at it. For the next week, I'll come in your mouth before each meal. If I suspect you're not showing the proper submissive enthusiasm, then that will be your meal."

They started the next morning. Because Alana couldn't kneel comfortably on her haunches with the brand still healing, Mark lay on the bed and had her crouch over him. His cock grew hard and large as she licked and kissed it. He allowed her to do most of the work, resisting his own impulse to fuck her face the way he usually did. She would have to earn this one. He allowed her to use her hands, one cupped sweetly around his balls, the other gripping the base as she guided his cock into her mouth.

Her lips closed in a red ring around his hard shaft. It felt so heavenly that Mark began to arch into her, thrusting slightly forward, despite his own promise to himself to let her do it all.

As he was nearing a fever pitch of pleasure, he completely abandoned any effort at self-control and grabbed her by the hair, forcing his cock deep into her throat. Alana apparently hadn't been prepared for this sudden action. As he shot his load, she jerked back, coughing and spluttering like a novice.

Quickly, she tried to recover herself, sucking his now spent but still erect cock back into her mouth, into her throat. But the damage was done. She had failed the first test. There was no question about it.

~*~

Alana lay under the kitchen table on her stomach while the Master ate his breakfast, food he'd had her prepare, but forbidden her to eat. Tears pricked her eyes as her mouth watered. She was so hungry. But there was only the acrid aftertaste of semen on her tongue.

"Excuse me, Sir? Permission to speak?" she dared.

"Hmm?" Mark's mouth was full.

"I'm very thirsty, Sir. Perhaps some water?"

"No. Nothing but semen till you learn to love it."

Alana suppressed the sigh that rose to her lips. Cradling her head in her arms, she tried to block out the heavenly smell of syrup, sausage and hot coffee. She would just have to try harder.

After breakfast, Mark went to work in his office, leaving Alana loosely chained on the bed. It was silly to feel so hungry from missing just one meal, but there it was. She hoped he would give her another chance before lunch.

The brand throbbed painfully, and she reached back gingerly to touch the gauze padding that covered the wound. She couldn't wait to see the brand. Would it look like the loops on her bracelets? Would it heal properly? She was truly marked now — she was property, branded like chattel.

The image shifted as she gazed inward. She saw herself dressed in the fine silk scarves of her harem dreams. The brand was visible beneath her sheer flowing skirts as she danced through a palace with mosaic ceilings and soft light, clasping hands with the other girls as they whirled.

Alana opened her eyes, aware she must have dozed off. She lay on her stomach. Mark was standing over her, gently pulling away the bandage on her ass. "It's looking really good," he assured her.

"Can I see?" she asked.

"No. I'll show you when I'm ready."

Chastened, Alana bit her lower lip. Her stomach gurgled, reminding her she was hungry.

As if reading her mind, Mark said, "Ready for lesson number two? I'm not really in the mood, so you'll have to get me there. You have permission to open my pants and do whatever it takes to make me hard." He stood impassively, his arms folded across his chest.

Alana shifted on the bed, still in the loose chains. It would be harder to please him in this position, with him standing beside the bed, but she would do her best. She unzipped his jeans and pulled out his cock, which was only semi-erect. She soon had him erect, his cock like silken steel in her hands.

Just as she opened her mouth to take in his length, Mark curled his fingers into her hair and yanked her head back suddenly. Alana gasped from the unexpected pain while still trying to focus her attention on his cock. She tried to pull her head forward to reach his shaft. He kept tight hold of her hair. "Go on," he said. "Suck my dick."

The only way she could reach his cock was to pull against his hard grip. She felt like her hair was being yanked out by the roots, but she managed to strain far enough forward to take him partially into her mouth.

To her relief, he let go of her hair with a contented sigh. Though the angle was difficult and not what she was used to, she licked and caressed him with all her skill and devotion. Soon he was moaning. His balls tightened in her cupped hand and she gently squeezed them as her tongue traced the vein along his cock.

Mark groaned, thrusting against her. As he came, he pulled back so the bitter jism gushed into her mouth, coating her tongue. Squeezing her eyes closed, she swallowed quickly, trying not to gag.

Mark pulled out and looked down with a judge's grim expression. "Better. But far from perfect. I know you're not used to doing it from this angle, but that's no excuse. What really pisses me off is that face you made, like you were eating shit. What the fuck was that about?"

"But, Sir. That's not fair. I…" Her words shriveled in her throat at his glare.

"No excuses, Alana. You fucked up. That's all there is to it. Now you'll pay the price."

She couldn't suppress the whimper that escaped at these words, as she realized she would not be eating lunch, either.

He reached into his nightstand and pulled out a roll of duct tape. "Not only did you make that awful face, you spoke without permission. This will help you remember to keep your mouth shut."

He hauled her to her feet and tore off a piece of the tape with his teeth. He pressed it firmly across her mouth.

"You look hot," he observed. He peeled off another piece and pressed it across one nipple. Then the other was covered, and he stood back to admire the effect. "Nice," he said with a mean smile. Then he tilted his head and asked, "Do you need to pee, darling?"

Alana nodded her head, surprised to realize she did, given that she'd had nothing to drink since the night before.

"Well, isn't that just a shame?" he said, his eyes glinting evilly. "Because you can't. That will be part of your punishment. But just to make sure—" He paused to rip off another, longer piece of tape with his teeth.

"Spread your legs," he barked.

Reluctantly, Alana did as she was told.

Mark pressed the duct tape between her legs, carefully avoiding the piercing that contained her jewelry. "There," he said, tossing the roll of tape onto the bed. "Now you can come watch me eat lunch."

Alana had difficulty walking with the tape sticking to her pussy lips. Fortunately, Mark allowed her to go slowly as he led her into the kitchen. Again, she was forced to lie on her stomach under the table.

Miserably, she cradled her head in her arms. Silent tears trickled down her cheeks as she lay, bladder full and stomach empty, while her cruel Master ate his sandwich, crunched on potato chips and slurped his drink.

When he was done, he helped her from beneath the table and had her stand in front of him. Gently, he wiped away her tears with his thumb. "My poor baby," he crooned. "I wish you would learn more quickly how to be a proper slut. Then I wouldn't have to do all these things to you. You do understand that, don't you, darling? That this is all your doing? If you took my come like you should, I wouldn't have to starve you, and tape your pretty cunt, now would I?"

His tone was solicitous, but she knew he didn't mean a word of it. No matter what she had done or how she had behaved, he would always find a way to punish her. "But you don't answer my direct question. Where are your manners, cunt girl?" He laughed. "Oh wait, you can't answer, can you? Not with that duct tape sealing your luscious mouth. Let me just take that off."

He gripped one edge of the tape and yanked it quickly away.

Alana's hands flew reflexively to her face. It stung but she barely noticed, so relieved to have the sticky, confining material off her mouth.

But the nipples were another story.

"Put your hands behind your back, gripping the elbows."

Reluctantly, Alana did as he commanded.

Cupping a breast in one hand, he peeled back a

corner of the tape. In one quick movement, he pulled it free from her skin. Alana gasped at the sudden pain, but at least it was over. The second nipple was worse, because she knew what to expect. As the tape was ripped from her flesh she cried out in pain, digging her fingers into her arms to keep her position. She longed to cover her sore nipples with her hands, but she didn't dare take them from behind her back.

"Very good, slave. You handled that well. Now for the final piece."

"Oh, please be careful!"

She hadn't meant to speak. It just slipped out. She knew that piece of duct tape would hurt far worse than the others when he tore it from her delicate skin. She began to tremble, though she managed to stay in position.

"How dare you direct me, cunt?" Mark demanded, his eyes flashing. "Do you want to make it ten times worse for yourself? Shall I starve you for another day? Shall I cover your entire body with tape and slowly rip it off until you're raw? Stand there and take it."

She bit back the whimper as he took hold of a corner of the sticky silver tape. He ripped it from her cunt, causing the gold hoop to sway against her thigh. The pain was blinding, and maybe it was because she was so hungry, or maybe it was because of the pain, but the ceiling tilted. Her mouth filled with saliva. Spots appeared before her eyes as the ringing started in her eyes. She felt her knees buckle, and she slipped gratefully away…

~*~

Winter was nearly over. Birds were trilling outside the window, singing in the trees. The sun was spilling out over puffy clouds, smearing the sky in golds and pinks. Mark stood in the bedroom doorway, watching Alana as she came awake. She stretched and sighed, falling back into the soft pillows.

"Good morning, beautiful girl," he said as she focused on his presence. "Today's the day. You've healed enough to see how the design will set permanently. I want you to see it." He held a large hand mirror, which he brought to the bedside.

Alana sat up expectantly. He knew she was very curious, even eager, to see what he had wrought upon her flesh with fire and steel. He released the loose bed chains and held the mirror as Alana positioned herself until she could see the brand.

Alana stared in fascination at the looped ovals seared into her skin.

Mark removed the mirror and sat down beside her. "Well, what do you think?"

She smiled at him, and though he looked for it, he couldn't see a trace of guile in her face. "It's amazing. It's as if someone carved it there. It's so perfect."

"Yes," Mark agreed happily. "Pretty good for a first attempt, if I say so myself."

It occurred to him that he'd like to show her off, to have someone in the world other than the two of them be a witness to what she had become — his perfect slave girl.

But of course that couldn't happen. As far as the world knew, she was dead — another mysterious disappearance in these tragic and uncertain times. As for him, he had no family to speak of, save for an estranged stepbrother he hadn't seen in nearly a decade. His few friends had fallen away over the two years of his obsession with the lovely Alana Hunter.

Could he really hope to keep her here forever? Did he even want to? Wouldn't he tire of this same woman? Of only her company?

No.

He would never tire of those deep blue eyes, so

expressive of her feelings. He would never tire of that soft, supple skin, those full, perfect breasts, those dusty rose nipples, that delicious cunt that molded so tightly around his hard cock. He would never tire of her lovely smile — so rarely flashed, but all the more special because of that. Or those long, shapely legs and slender ankles. He would never tire of her increasingly graceful submission. Of whipping that perfect flesh until she flew. Of using that perfect body until she came.

But in the end, he had her because he'd taken her. He'd stolen her and held her in chains and fear. Yes, it was true there had been a shift over the past month — her submission seemed genuine, her passion authentic. But was that enough?

He had ripped her from the life she knew — the fame and fortune of being a movie star. He had forced her to submit. He had taken her against her will and kept her in chains. Did it matter that he had done it with passion, with love? Did it matter that every moment of his life he was consumed by her, by thoughts of her, by a need for her that was overpowering?

He claimed that he loved her, but had he ever given her a chance to respond in kind? He demanded her submission. He took what he wanted of her. But had he ever given her a choice?

Yet, how could he? If he gave her a choice — if he opened the door and said stay or go, she would surely choose that which would take her from him.

Then he would have nothing. No reason for continuing. She was his essence, and without her, he would dissolve, disappear without a trace.

That brought him back to the issue of love. He could possess her body forever. He could keep her here, bind her tighter, whip her harder, subjugate her more completely. But could he ever hope to win her heart? No matter how obediently she behaved, he could never compel her to love him.

All at once, though he'd known it on some level from the moment he'd first hatched the insane idea to abduct her, the realization she could never love him *freely* had become intolerable to him.

"Sir?" Alana's sexy, husky voice recalled him back to the moment. "Is everything okay, Mark?"

Mark.

God, he loved it when she used his name, which she so rarely did.

He regarded her for a long moment. Was the concern in her voice and her expression genuine, or just born out of fear?

"Not really," he admitted.

Her face crumpled. "Oh, Sir. I'm sorry, Sir. Did I—"

"No, no," he said abruptly. "It's nothing you did."

All at once, he knew what he had to do. He had known it all along, hadn't he?

Before he lost his resolve, he got up from the bed and went into the closet. He selected a silky blue dress he knew would look beautiful on her sexy curves, and a pair of leather shoes with a low heel. Going to the bureau, he opened the drawer that contained the lace and silk undergarments he sometimes had her wear. He removed a pair of white lace panties and a matching bra that clasped in the front.

He lay them on the bed.

She looked from the clothing to him, her unspoken question on her face.

"You may shower and dress on your own," he said without further explanation. "Put on these things and present yourself to me when you're ready." He turned and left the room.

~*~

Alana sat up and reached for the pretty dress. She fingered the silky fabric as she tried to figure out what was going on. The dress was something she would have worn in the before time. It was well-tailored, the design simple but elegant. Usually when he chose an outfit, it was something a prostitute would wear, complete with garters, sheer stockings, stiletto heels and corset. Bra and panties? Never.

She climbed out of bed and hurried to the bathroom to use the toilet and wash up. She moved quickly, not wishing to make her Master wait any longer than necessary. She was wildly curious about whatever new game he had devised for her, and only hoped it was something she could handle with reasonable grace and courage.

Back in the bedroom, she put on the bra, which fit perfectly. As she pulled the silky panties up, the heavy golden hoop nestled against her. She liked the feel of it, hidden in her panties, the metal warming against her flesh. She pulled the dress over her head and stepped into the shoes.

She left the bedroom and walked down the hall, past the study, which she could see was empty, and into the living room.

Mark was sitting on the couch staring out the window, a brooding look on his face that made her stomach lurch unpleasantly. As she approached, she racked her brain, trying to think what she might have done to displease him.

She started to kneel on the floor at his feet, but to her surprise, he gestured toward the cushion beside him. "Here, sit here next to me."

It was all so peculiar. The clothing and shoes, the use of the furniture, as if she were a regular person and not his slave, his possession.

"Alana, we need to talk. I've been doing a lot of thinking." He looked, she realized with a small shock, nervous. He bit his lip and twisted his hands in his lap before finally speaking again. "I don't know how to begin. I don't know what to say." Mark looked at her, his eyes almost pleading.

What did he want from her? Was this some kind of terrible new game? What were the rules? Would she be able to learn them quickly enough to avoid punishment?

He looked away again, out the window. Finally, he turned back to her. "Alana. I love you." He blew out a breath. "When I stole you away — when I abducted you — it was my intention to keep you forever, no matter what it took. I've held you here against your will. I told myself it didn't matter to me. Just having you here was enough."

What the hell was he saying? Was it no longer enough? Alana sat still, trying to keep the sudden fear from showing on her face. Was this it, then? Was he going to kill her at last?

No, don't be crazy, she admonished herself. *He loves you.* She willed herself to be calm as she waited for him to continue.

He took a breath. "I find I no longer want to be your jailer, Alana. I'm no longer satisfied with your servitude under duress. It is no longer enough to accept your submission, when I know it's not freely given."

Alana had begun to tremble, and she impulsively dropped from the couch to the floor and wrapped her arms around her Master's knees. "Please, I don't know what I did, Sir, but please give me another chance!" she begged. "Don't kill me, Sir. Please, I'll do better, I promise. Whatever you want — whatever you need, Sir — I'll do it." She burst into tears.

Strong arms lifted her up. "No, no, Alana, no!" he said, his tone urgent. "I don't want to kill you. Christ, I'd rather kill myself than take the light that is you out of the world." His voice cracked.

With her head buried against his chest, she couldn't see his face, but it sounded as if he were crying. Which was impossible. Mark was always in control—always.

She looked up at him, shocked to see a tear rolling down his cheek. Impulsively, she reached up and wiped it away, as he had done for her so many times before.

"I'm sorry, Alana. I'm not expressing myself well. You're wonderful. You've done nothing wrong. You've learned to submit with real grace and obedience, and you're everything a man could want in a woman." He sighed. "But it's not enough. Because of what I've done, because I've taken you by force, I can never really know if your submission is fueled solely by fear. I didn't use to care. I told myself it didn't matter—that I had to have you, no matter the terms. But I can't keep pretending. It isn't working anymore. I need more. I need a reciprocal love."

Still confused and desperate to figure out the rules to this strange, dangerous new game, Alana again tried to assure him of her obedience, but he stopped her with a finger to her lips.

"Listen to me. I've come to a decision that has been a long time in coming. I'm not sure what finally got me to this point. I think maybe it was the way you responded to the branding. You couldn't have feigned such a sincere response, even a great actress like you."

He touched her cheek, his eyes so sad. "What I mean is, I think you have developed an understanding of the life, of this lifestyle of Master and slave, of Dominant and submissive. But you've only experienced it through force. Through bondage, conditioning and enslavement, without choice, without free will. It should be enough for me. I thought it was enough for me. But not anymore. I can't do it." His voice cracked again and he stopped speaking.

Alana sat frozen. She still didn't understand what he was saying, though she tried to cling to his claim that he didn't want to kill her. Then her blood turned to ice in her veins. He didn't *want* to kill her, but what choice did he have? He couldn't possibly set her free and risk her turning him in to the authorities. He would have no choice.

It was enough for me. But not anymore. I can't do it.

He must be saying he was tired of her. And if that were the case, he would have to kill her, and possibly himself as well. She was as good as dead.

She began to cry softly, her face hidden in her hands.

"Alana, please don't cry." He pulled her again into his arm. "Why are you shaking?"

"I don't want to die, Sir. Please, Mark. Give me another chance."

He held her at arms length and stared into her eyes. "Stop that," he ordered. "I am not going to kill you. I'm going to let you go."

She was so startled by his words that she stopped crying, her mouth falling open. "What?"

"That's right," he said emphatically. "I know there's the risk you'll turn me in to the police, and who could blame you? But even if you do, they won't find me. I won't be here. I know how to disappear. And anyway, I don't care about that. What I'm saying, my beloved darling, is I can claim your body, and I can keep you forever, but I can't make you love me. I can't make your heart feel something it won't. And I don't want you anymore, without that."

Alana was dumbfounded. Did he mean it? Or was this another test, a sadistic trick?

Mark was watching her. Whatever he saw in her face seemed to cause him pain, but doggedly he went on. "Here's my plan. I know I can't just thrust you back into the world, as you are now. I'm going to help you decompress. I'm going to allow you time to 'get back to normal'." He put air quotes around the words with his fingers. "From this moment, you no longer belong to me. You will sleep in the guest bedroom. You will have your clothing. You will no longer submit to me or be subject to control or punishment. You will be here as my guest. You will eat with me at the table. You will take back your body. You will decide what you wear and how you spend your day, as long as it's in this house."

Was this real? Was it really happening? Alana knew she should be whooping with joy, but she only felt numb.

"At the end of the week," he continued, "assuming you've made good progress, I'll take you away from here. I can't drop you off in the city, for obvious reasons, but I'll give you money and leave you somewhere where you'll be able to get yourself home." His voice cracked, and he choked out the rest of the words. "It's over, Alana. It's done. You're free."

He stood abruptly and, without another glance at her, fled from the room.

Alana sat on the couch staring down at her hands. She fingered the iron bracelets at her wrists, still not entirely sure this wasn't just another elaborate ruse, another dangerous, cruel game.

But the tears, that stricken look on his face. Was

he serious? Would he really set her free? She thought of her family, who had to believe she was dead at this point. What would it be like to return to them, to reclaim her life, her career?

And Mark. What would become of him? She would never see him again, of that she was certain. He couldn't risk that. He would vanish, or be caught. Then there would be the trial, and certain jail for him—a life sentence, he now the one behind bars…

At the sound of footsteps, she looked up. Mark entered the room, his mouth set in a grim line. He held a small key in his hand. "Hold out your wrists," he directed.

As she did so, he inserted the key into the small opening at the clasp on the bracelet on her right wrist. The mechanism sprang free and the two ovals parted. He repeated the procedure on the other wrist. Then, kneeling before his slave, he did the same with each ankle cuff.

Alana touched the skin at her wrists, which felt naked and strange.

"Stand up and take off your panties."

Alana rose to her feet and lifted her dress. As she tugged down the underwear, he pulled a tiny pair of jeweler's pliers from his jeans pocket, and she understood what he was going to do. She almost protested. She found to her own surprise that she didn't want him to remove the gold hoop. She wanted to keep it. It was hers.

But she didn't dare say no. Even though he claimed to have given her back that right, she found she was incapable of refusing. Perhaps that would come in time. This was all so new, so uncertain.

If Mark was aware of her discomfiture, he gave no sign. Crouching in front of her, he sprung the lock on the small oval of gold that hung so prettily from her pussy. "There," he said, looking up at her. "You're free."

Alana lay sprawled diagonally in the bed, no chains, no cuffs, no Mark. It was strange, though not unpleasant to sleep in the guest bedroom by herself. As she came fully awake, she stroked her bare wrists, feeling the absence of the iron that had been a constant.

She had slept fitfully, a part of her waiting to be awakened by a blow, or a sting of the lash, or a stiff cock thrusting at her lips or invading her cunt or ass. On some level, she was still waiting for the game to be up, and for the retribution that would surely follow.

But it was morning, and he hadn't come to her. She could smell coffee brewing. She sat up and slid her feet over the edge of the bed, letting them rest on the soft throw rug. It was warm enough now that she didn't need a robe, but she liked the idea that she *could* use one if she wished. So she reached over to where she had placed the robe on the end of the bed, and wrapped it around her body, enjoying the feel of the soft silk on her skin.

After washing up in her own bathroom, she ventured out into the living room. She could hear Mark moving about in the kitchen, and the tantalizing smell of frying bacon assailed her.

"Good morning," Mark called out to her.

"Good morning, Sir," she replied as she came into the kitchen. It wouldn't have occurred to her to greet him first. She had been trained for too long in the art of silence.

"Have a seat at the table. I'm just making some scrambled eggs."

Alana smiled uncertainly. Her kneeling cushion by his chair was gone. She'd been next to the table, on it, under it. She had never actually sat down at it. She slid awkwardly onto the chair, feeling faintly ridiculous, like an imposter.

Mark hovered around her, setting down a plate of eggs and bacon, pouring her coffee, stirring in the sugar and cream he knew she liked. Alana sat staring at the food.

Mark soon came and sat across from her, his own plate piled high. He took a swallow of coffee and reached for the salt. "Eat while it's hot. Aren't you hungry?" His tone was jovial, if a little forced.

After a moment he said quietly, "What is it, Alana? What's the matter?"

Alana, who had been staring down at her plate, lifted her head. "I'm sorry, Sir. I haven't even used a fork for so long. I'm just not used to this. I'm-I'm afraid," she admitted.

Mark furrowed his brow. "Afraid of what? The food's not poisoned, if that's what you're thinking. Look, I'm eating it." He shoveled in a large bite of eggs into his mouth.

She didn't dare articulate her fear. That he was setting her up. That he would punish her the minute she dared to use a fork and eat like an equal, instead of kneeling at his feet, her mouth open like a baby, waiting for his offering.

Mark studied her for a while longer, comprehension dawning on his face. "You don't trust me," he said slowly. "That's it, isn't it? You don't trust me not to betray you. To go back on the deal that you are free this week, free to do whatever you like, except leave. You think I'm setting you up so I can punish you, cage you, make you suffer for your trust."

His voice sounded sad. When she didn't deny it, he said, "I'm sorry you can't trust me. I can't even blame you. But the deal stands. I'm going to help you take back yourself." He pointed toward her plate. "Eat. If you still require it, you have my permission to eat. Use the fork. Use the knife and spoon. Eat until you are satisfied. Take your time." He said it gently. His eyes were still sad but his expression was kind.

Alana relaxed a little. Hesitantly, she picked up the fork.

She ate a small bite of the eggs. Nothing happened. She dared a sip of the coffee and still Mark calmly ate his own food. She took another bite of egg and picked up a piece of crisp bacon. The food was delicious. The freedom was strange but not unpleasant. She ate the rest of her meal, casting sidelong glances at Mark as she did so.

Whatever game he was playing, she hoped she

would learn the rules fast.

Normally after breakfast, Mark would groom his slave girl. She would sit obediently on the bathroom counter while he carefully shaved her underarms, her legs, and finally her pussy. Usually afterwards, he would make her come, or fuck her right there on the counter.

Today, after breakfast Mark went into his study. "I have a little work to do," he said. "If you wouldn't mind cleaning up?"

Alana was glad for something to do, and she happily cleaned the kitchen and washed the dishes. Then she found herself at a loss. Should she groom herself? He had said he wasn't going to use her sexually any more, so what was the point? Unless it was another test?

Not sure what to do, Alana chose a murder mystery from one of the shelves in the living room. With her new freedom, Mark had given her full reign of the house, including the use of the TV and his vast library of books, both fiction and nonfiction.

A window had been cracked in the living room, a pleasant, cool breeze wafting into the room. She could push that window all the way open. She could climb out right now and run down the road.

Of course, he might realize she was missing before she got away, but that was unlikely. He rarely came out of his study in less than an hour. That would give her enough time to escape.

She could go.

And yet she didn't.

It was too risky. There would be a trap. Better to wait, to bide her time.

She curled up in a chair and opened the book to page one.

That night Mark suggested she make the dinner, something she'd never done without his express participation and direction. She was wearing a pink blouse and a pair of blue jeans, the clothing still unfamiliar against her skin. Alone in the kitchen, she could have grabbed a sharp knife and used it on her captor, but she didn't. She thought about his gun, which she hadn't seen, she realized, in quite some time.

But she didn't want to kill Mark.

She wanted to cook, something she had used to enjoy doing, in the before time.

Mark kept a well-stocked freezer and pantry,

and Alana found everything she needed to prepare beef goulash with carrots, mushrooms and fresh herbs. She made a pan of cornbread to complement the spice of the goulash. They shared a bottle of Cabernet, and Mark toasted the meal with a raise of his glass.

"I had no idea you were such an accomplished cook, Alana. This is delicious."

Alana smiled, warmed by his praise.

After supper they sat on the couch together in the living room. Again, it felt strange. She wasn't used to being treated as Mark's equal. To her surprise, she wasn't entirely sure that she liked it. Normally she would have been naked at his feet. He might suddenly pull her up and onto his lap so he could stroke her. Or tell her to go to the playroom and prepare for a session.

She would dutifully obey, waiting patiently in the middle of the room if he had told her to, or kneeling, her ass raised high, her forehead resting on the white floor, her heart beating in anticipation.

He would enter a while later, and the erotic torture would begin. The cane, his cock, the whip, the cross, the suspension rack, whatever pleased him. Whatever he decreed.

She would lose track of time and space as she became pure, raw sensation. Pain and pleasure would blend and bleed, twist and spiral inside her until she dissolved into it — into him.

Alana reread the same paragraph in her book a dozen times, and still the words didn't register.

"A penny for your thoughts."

Alana looked up at the sound of his voice. He was staring at her, an intensity in his gaze.

"Nothing," she replied reflexively. *Everything*.

He pursed his lips. As his slave, she didn't have the right to withhold anything from her Master, not even her thoughts.

But she wasn't his slave.

According to this odd, new situation, she was his guest.

As if having the same thoughts, Mark nodded slowly, saying nothing more. Instead, he rose to his feet, stretching elaborately. "I think I'll turn in early. I'm really tired."

She let him go, of course. It was a relief, in a way, to have him gone. She didn't have to sit on the couch any longer in her clothing pretending to read her book, wondering how to behave.

She got up and went into "her" bathroom. She stripped out of her clothes and stared at herself in the mirror, turning around and twisting back to admire the brand. He had taken her slave jewelry, but he couldn't take that from her.

Turning back, she noticed the shadow of stubble on her mons. She touched the soft fuzz and realized with a small shock that she liked being smooth. She had grown accustomed to the bare, silken feel.

Looking furtively at the closed bathroom door, she decided she would do it herself. Even if he no longer wanted her, she would keep herself ready. She would keep herself soft and bare for him, just in case he changed his mind. And if it was a test, she would pass it, when he inevitably called an end to this odd game they were playing.

He had filled the drawers with all the toiletries she would need, including a fresh razor and shaving cream. She drew a bath and placed the razor and cream on the ledge. Climbing in, she soaked for a while, luxuriating in the hot water. Then, trying to imitate his long, even strokes, she shaved her legs, then her underarms, and finally her pussy.

He did it better. She missed his sure touch.

Alana dried her body and applied the creams

and oils he used to smooth into her flesh. Then she quickly washed her face, brushed her teeth and went into the bedroom.

Sleep eluded her as she tried to get comfortable in the soft bed. Where were her bracelets and chains? Where was the strong, warm man she had become used to having beside her, holding her close until she fell asleep?

Her hand found its way to the brand. She traced the slightly raised lines, visualizing the linked ovals. She had been branded by the man who would now set her free.

She would never feel the lash again. Never again know the intensity of being cropped on her spread pussy and being ordered to come. Never know the humiliation of crouching naked while her Master urinated on her back, the yellow droplets rolling down her sides and hanging for a second in perfect globes at her nipples, before sliding down to the cold porcelain below her.

She should be thrilled he was going to set her free. She could go back to the before time, when she was in command — in control. She could return to the filming and the photo shoots, to the runway events and the promo tours, to the hectic, glamorous, exciting life that had been hers.

Did she miss it?

Could you miss a dream?

What was real now?

What did she want?

What would happen when she told everyone what had happened to her? Would they even believe it? She had been whipped and tortured and completely isolated from all other human contact. She had been pierced and branded. She had submitted to it all. She hadn't really tried to fight him, had she? Would they understand she had been held here against her will? That she had had no choice but to comply?

What would they make of it all? How would she be treated? Would they believe her wild tales? And where was the man who had done these horrible things? If they tracked him down, despite his certainty they wouldn't, he would be tried. She would be on trial as well, with the whole world avidly watching. The star witness.

She would be forced to testify for the record, for the world, about her punishments, about the cage. Would her brand be entered as evidence? Her piercing? It was all too horrible to contemplate.

Well, if she did go, she would face that

particular hurdle when she came to it.

What was she thinking? *If* she went? Of course she was going. She had to go. Didn't she?

"I can't make you love me."

She fell asleep finally, cupping her pussy as if it were Mark's hand there, keeping her safe, keeping her wet for him. That night her dreams weren't about harem girls in foreign lands.

This time she dreamed of Mark.

Chapter 12

They shared meals, sitting across from each other at the table like any couple. They exchanged small talk about the books they were reading, or the weather. Neither brought up the subject of her impending departure. Alana didn't have the courage, and Mark, it seemed, didn't have the heart.

Alana began to get comfortable again on the furniture. She became used to wearing clothing. Her fingers searched less frequently for the bracelets that were no longer there.

He never called for her and never came to her bedroom at night. Still, just in case, she continued to keep her pussy shaved.

After being so conditioned with constant sex, constant punishment, and constant attention, Alana felt lost. And lonely. Her body ached for his attentions. She found the only way to settle herself to sleep was to masturbate.

At first she hesitated, uncomfortable and still
not totally sure it was permitted. Then it became
her solace. She would rub and finger-fuck herself,
staying as quiet as she could when she came. The
climaxes barely scratched her itch, but they were
better than nothing.

One day when Mark was ensconced in his
study, she crept into the playroom. Everything was
in its place — the ropes, whips and chains hung
along the walls, the St. Andrew's cross, the
whipping chair, the suspension bar. The shades
had been drawn, the place shrouded in shadow.
Not sure she should be in there at all, Alana
slipped over to the toy chest and opened it. Inside
were the myriad of dildos, clips, clamps, coiled
rope, duct tape and lubricants.

Looking guiltily over her shoulder, Alana
grabbed a battery-operated vibrator. Shutting the
lid of the toy chest, she fled from the room. That
night she fucked herself with the phallus, silently
begging her Master for permission to come as it
took her over the edge.

As the week passed, Alana began to play with
herself during the day as well. She really hadn't
much else to do. Her time when she had been
Mark's slave had been spent chained, bound,
cuffed, tortured or adored, always serving him in

some way. Mark didn't have cable, and anyway, she had never much liked television. He hadn't given her access to the internet, and there was only so much reading she could do.

When Mark was working, she would slip into her bedroom, keeping her ear cocked for any sound that he was coming. She would slip her hand into her panties and bring herself to a rapid release. Though unbidden, the images in her mind as she brought herself to orgasm always included Mark. Scenes from their time together powered her fantasies—the torture, the tenderness, the whippings and the kisses intertwined.

As the week drew to a close, her courage increased, along with an undefined anxiety. She tried to bring up the subject of her leaving. Mark refused to discuss it. He had made his decision. She would be set free. She would return to her life, he assured her, and he would rebuild his.

~*~

Mark behaved calmly with her, betraying little emotion. There was no repeat episode of the first evening, no humiliating tears. His pride wouldn't allow it.

He argued endlessly with himself about his decision. Why had he meddled with something so perfect? He'd had her just where he wanted her — at his feet, at his mercy. Yet he knew he had no choice. It was no longer enough to keep her in chains.

There was no going back. The die was cast.

Tomorrow morning he would drive her to a bus station in a nearby town. He'd already arranged to sell the house and all its contents (except the toys and gear in the playroom and basement, which would go directly to the municipal dump).

He had his fake passport and access to several overseas bank accounts that would provide him with all he needed for a long time to come. By the time the authorities descended, he would be halfway round the world, with a new identity and a new life.

A life without her, without meaning.

He told himself to stop being melodramatic. His life didn't hinge on her. That was ridiculous. He could disappear into oblivion and find another slave girl. This time a willing one, one who yearned to submit without being forced.

But she wouldn't be Alana. She wouldn't be *his* Alana.

Not touching her all week had been the hardest

thing he'd ever done in his life. He'd held himself back only through sheer grit and determination. To have her so close and not touch her, kiss her, fuck her, whip her, adore her, had been a living hell, one he'd imposed on himself.

But beneath his cool exterior, his heart was breaking.

His lust raged unchecked. He could hold it no longer. He had to claim her at least once more. He needed to taste her sweet lips, to feel her hot cunt, to make her suffer for him one last time.

~*~

Alana stood at the window in her room, watching the last splash of color fade from the sky. She wore a short dress with a batik pattern of fish and seashells in deep ink blue. Mark really had an eye for elegant simplicity. She hadn't bothered with a bra or panties, and her feet were bare.

Her own clothes, the things she'd arrived in, were laid out for tomorrow. He told her she would take nothing of his with her — none of the beautiful clothing, nor the strange jewelry she'd worn at her wrists, ankles and sex. She touched her bottom through the material of the dress. He couldn't take that back. His mark would always remind her of this strange time.

Lost in a daydream, she didn't hear anyone enter the room, but suddenly Mark was behind her, his hands gripping her shoulders, his scent enveloping her. "Don't move."

Her heart kicked instantly into overdrive.

Was this when he admitted it had all been a game? A trap? She could barely breathe.

She started to turn around, to sink to her knees, but his hands tightened, the fingers digging painfully into her flesh. "I said *don't move.*"

Alana froze. While a part of her was terrified, she couldn't help but feel a kind of elation. He still wanted her! She was his adored, cherished slave girl.

Her thoughts were cut short as he spoke, his voice low and urgent. "Put your hands up against the window. High up."

Alana obeyed, pressing her palms against the cool glass as she tried to get air into her lungs. His large hands slid underneath her dress and ran along her sides, sending a shiver of raw desire through her loins. She couldn't control the whimper of desire when his fingers closed over her nipples. He rolled and twisted them until they were engorged and throbbing. Then he slid his hands down her stomach to her cunt. He cupped the smooth mons and pressed a finger inside.

Alana groaned.

He ground his palm against her clit, and Alana moaned her pleasure. Before long, she began to tremble, a climax hurtling through her body in shuddering waves. Her knees began to buckle and she pressed her hands hard against the windowpane for support.

"Oh, god," she moaned, trying to form the words she knew her Master required, "Please, may I—?"

He cut her off, "Don't ask me for anything," he said gruffly. "Don't ask permission—it's no longer mine to give."

Alana was too far-gone, too close to release to fully process the import of his words. She let her orgasm lift and carry her as his fingers continued their perfect, relentless dance against her sex.

As she sagged against the window, Alana felt Mark's naked body press against hers, warm and strong. Gripping her shoulders, he turned her toward him. He was naked, his cock hard and fully erect.

As her arms fell to her sides, he slipped the

dress from her shoulders, and it puddled to the floor at her feet. He stared down into her eyes. "I have to have you, at least once more."

His voice was commanding. Gone was the almost timorous man she had experienced during this long, strange week. Her Master had returned to her.

Moving her from the window, Mark pressed her against the wall and hoisted her onto his hips. As she wrapped her legs around him, he eased her onto his shaft. Her cunt clamped around his thick cock as it filled her completely, an after-spasm from her recent orgasm making her jerk against him.

For a moment, Mark just held her, his face resting against her bare breasts, his strong arms encircling her. Then he lifted and lowered her on his cock, as if she weighed nothing. He began to thrust faster, his steady, perfect rhythm reawakening her need. He began to pant, his head thrown back, his face suffused with lust.

Impulsively she wrapped her arms around him, dropping her head to his shoulder as he pummeled her into ecstasy.

~*~

Neither spoke as they pushed around the food

on their plates. Mark stole a glance at the girl of his dreams, the woman he was sending away. She was dressed in the clothing she'd worn when he'd abducted her—the bright yellow sweater and faded jeans, her feet shod in expensive boots.

How he yearned to take her in his arms. To kiss her hair and tell her how much he loved her. If he stood up now and took it all back, if he rescinded her right to leave, informed her she would remain here forever, bound to him as slave to Master until death did them part, would she accept it? And if she did, what would it mean?

Ironically, he had achieved the goal he'd set for himself when he'd first abducted her. She had come to accept her lot as his sexual property. But he knew better. She was like those hostages who became unnaturally attached to their captors. She might think she wanted to stay, but it was fear and conditioning, not love, that motivated her behavior.

It was time.

He pushed back from the table and stood. "Let's go."

Silently, Alana stood as well. For a moment it seemed she would speak, but she said nothing. It was still early, the sun just peeking up over the mountains as they stepped outside together.

Mark opened the door of his car and motioned for her to get in back. "I'm going to blindfold you so you aren't tempted to remember the way back. You will lie down flat on the seat. If you try to get up, I'll tie you down, understand?"

Mutely, she nodded. There were tears in her eyes.

Once she lay down on the back seat, he slipped a sleep mask over her face. She didn't move or protest. Satisfied, he closed her door and slid into the driver's seat.

They drove in silence for close to an hour. Alana remained as still and silent as death in the backseat. Mark held the steering wheel in a white-knuckled grip. As he pulled at last into the bus station, his heart felt so heavy he thought it might crush him from the inside.

"Sit up," he said, as he pulled into a parking space at the back of the empty lot. He turned off the ignition and climbed into the back seat next to Alana. He helped her to a sitting position as he removed the sleep mask.

As she blinked in the sunlight, he handed her an envelope. "There's five hundred dollars in there. That should be plenty to get you back to the city or wherever you're going."

Alana looked at him, her large violet-blue eyes again pooling with tears. "What's that?" She pointed to the numbers written neatly in the center of the envelope.

"It's my cell. In case you needed to contact me. It will be a working number for the next twenty-four hours. After that you won't be able to reach me. Ever."

Heat rushed into his face. As if she would ever want to reach him for anything ever, except to lead the police to him. He climbed out of the car and gestured for her to get out. "Go on. Go, before I change my mind."

~*~

Alana sat in the bus station, her purse in her lap. She'd bought a ticket for New York City, but she hadn't called anyone yet. Not her parents, not her agent, not the police. She'd watched as Mark drove away, feeling strangely as if he were taking a part of her with him.

She stared down at the ticket. The bus would be arriving in forty minutes.

She should have been thinking about her future, about her freedom, but all she could think of was his face the last time he'd looked at her — the pain and sorrow in those green-gold eyes, and the way he'd kept clenching and unclenching his hands.

She shifted on the hard bench as her body recalled his touch. She could almost feel his large, hard cock sliding inside her, his hands on her throat, her breasts, her ass — possessing her completely, possessing her as no one ever had before.

What would sex be like now, without the overlay of dominance and forced submission? While he had truly frightened her, even terrorized her with his brutal behavior, she couldn't deny he had also made her feel wildly alive. Pleasure and pain had been woven skillfully over and around her for so long, she no longer knew if she could experience one without the other.

Alana glanced up at the large clock on the wall. Soon she would be on her way. She would call her parents when she got back to the city.

What would life be like now? She would be thrust back into the limelight, bombarded by the media, surrounded by people who were intrigued with her fame and her supposed beauty, ghoulishly obsessed with what had happened to her during these bizarre months of forced captivity. None of them knew her at all. They never had.

No lover before Mark had ever tapped into her latent submissive sexuality or been able to release her fierce passion. Despite what he'd done to her, or perhaps partially because of it, she felt more alive in his arms than at any other time.

She shook her head. This was insane. She was still brainwashed. His hold on her would fade as she acclimated to the real world.

As the minutes ticked by, she sat quietly, her mind drifting.

Mark.

Sir.

She looked down at the envelope with the number printed neatly in the center. There was an old pay phone beneath the clock. Would it even work?

Alana reached into her purse for a quarter.

Chapter 1

Callie flopped onto her bed around midnight, wiped out. There were still a ton of boxes to unpack, not to mention pictures to hang and groceries to buy, but she'd earned a rest.

She reached for her laptop and pulled up her emails. She had twenty-seven new messages waiting on DomZone—the BDSM dating site she'd recently discovered. Would she really have the nerve to meet one of those guys someday? To find out if BDSM was something more than just a masturbatory fantasy? Probably not, but it was fun to explore, especially from the safety of her new apartment.

She navigated to the site and clicked on her profile. She updated her location, a thrill of excitement moving through her for the hundredth time that week. She was in the big city and would soon start her dream job at the museum. After graduating from college and working for a few years in various dead-end jobs at art galleries in Milwaukee, her real life was beginning at last.

A quick scan of the messages showed the usual assortment of skeevy horndogs sniffing around for someone to jerk off with over the internet. Most of them could barely string together a coherent sentence. And *why* did men think women liked disembodied dick pics?

No, thank you.

She returned to the front page of the DomZone site and noticed a new tab: *Abduction Fantasies Explored.*

The abduction fantasy page had a number of links, each one leading to a different chat room based on your particular fetish. She perused the list that catered to the Dom/sub heterosexual crowd, her panties moistening as she examined the choices.

Swashbuckling Pirate Island

Daddy's Naughty Little Girl

Slave Planet

Evil Boss

Bought by a Billionaire

A shiver of delicious fear moved through her body. She closed her eyes, for a moment imagining a gorgeous, sexy Dom whisking her away to his secret BDSM mansion, where he would hold her captive in a lavish dungeon filled with restraint devices and plenty of rope and chain.

Of course, just like in the books she read, he would start out as the stern Master, but he wouldn't be able to help himself. He would fall head-over-heels in love with his beautiful slave girl. He would lift her gently from her confines and carry her to his huge bed. He would whisper that he was as enslaved to her in love as she was to him. He would shower her with jewels and kisses, and beg her to be his forever…

Callie clicked on the link and entered the chat room. There were about a dozen people there. She watched for a while as conversations scrolled by, with people discussing various fantasies and engaging in some role play. One guy kept using all caps and shouting at every female in the room to get on her knees and worship his cock.

With a snort, Callie started to click away from the room. Just before her finger pressed the key, the pinging sound of someone sending her a private message caught her attention. She glanced at the name, surprised to see the message was from *SexKitten312*. In her brief time on the site, it had always been guys who tried to private message. But there was a small (f) next to the user name, which indicated a female with a submissive orientation.

Curious, Callie accepted the message request and

read the message.

"Hi, SubAngel. I noticed you're from the Chicago area, like me! Just wanted to say hi."

Callie clicked on SexKitten's profile. She was female, aged twenty-seven—two years older than Callie, and was seeking a "real life Master to claim her completely—heart, body and soul."

So why was she messaging Callie?

Not wanting to be rude, Callie typed back, *"Hi. I'm actually new to Chicago, and to this website."*

"Wow, what a coincidence. I'm new to the area too. Originally from Texas. I love going to the clubs and scening with hot Doms. I can't wait to explore the scene here in the Windy City."

"There were some BDSM groups where I went to college, but I never really checked them out," Callie offered.

She glanced at the main chat area. The guy writing in all caps was now ordering every "sub slut" in the room to "spread her legs and show him her cunt."

"Jeez, that dude is so lame," SexKitten typed in the private message box. *"I can't stand guys like that. They just don't get it."*

"Agreed," Callie replied, warming to the girl. It *would* be nice to meet someone her own age in this new city, especially someone who may have some actual experience with BDSM.

They chatted for a while in the private message tab, making fun of the various guys in the chat room, and sharing a little about their lives. Callie learned that Diana — her real name — had graduated from Texas Tech with a degree in nursing, and had moved to Chicago for her work and because she had family there.

"I have an older cousin here," Diana typed. *"His name is Damon. He found my stash of BDSM romance novels under my bed the summer I turned fourteen."*

"OMG. You must have died of embarrassment!"

"No, he was really cool about it. He assured me it was nothing to be ashamed of. Turns out, he's into the scene too! He's promised to take me around to all the cool BDSM clubs, now that I'm living here. I can't wait!"

"Sweet," Callie typed back, a little jealous. It would be nice to have someone to introduce her into the scene. She was ready, at last, to explore in real life what had always been just a sexual fantasy.

"So, what's your experience in the scene?" Diana typed.

"I don't really have any actual experience in BDSM. I'm still kind of exploring at this point. I like the idea of a strong, dominant man having his way with me. Keeping me captive in an opulent dungeon filled with silk pillows and sexy chains… You know, typical romance novel stuff, I guess…"

"Way cool," Diana replied. *"Billionaire Master fantasies are hot."*

"Right? I've read a few of those novels, but they're always so unrealistic. Who ever heard of a twenty-five-year-old billionaire?"

"You'd be surprised. Anyway, I have to go now, but let's connect in real life. My email is DianaJohnson3773@gmail.com. What's yours?"

Callie hesitated before responding. Was she ready to give her email to someone she'd chatted with for a few minutes on a BDSM sex site? On the other hand, it would be nice to connect with a new friend her first week in town. And Diana seemed fun.

Callie typed back her email address.

"Terrific." Diana texted. *"Talk soon!"*

Callie signed off soon after. She lay back with a satisfied sigh.

A new city. A new job. A potential new girlfriend. It seemed everything in her new life was falling nicely into place.

Over the next few days, Callie and Diana exchanged several texts and emails. One of Diana's fantasies freaked Callie out with its dark and graphic nature. The email read:

I fantasize about a guy holding me captive in his secret villa. He's incredibly gorgeous and wealthy, naturally. But he's also a very exacting taskmaster. I have to do everything he says, or I'm severely punished. Sometimes he puts me in a little cage and only lets me out when he wants to whip or fuck me.

At first, I'm terrified and resistant, but I soon learn that it's better to obey. He helps me to understand I'm just a worthless cunt who exists solely to please and amuse him.

My Master becomes my world. I am his property. He is Sir, and I would do anything to please him. No matter what he asks of me, I am happy to do it. I will wallow naked in the mud for his friends, if that amuses him. I will worship every inch of his body with my tongue. I allow myself to be on display at his parties. If he chooses to give me to a stranger on the street for an hour or a day, I have no choice but to obey.

When he takes me back, he punishes me for being with another man. If I dare to protest, I will be put in the cage and left there alone for hours or days… When he finally lets me out, I am so grateful I kiss his feet as my tears of gratitude fall…

The email went on like that for a while. Callie found herself both horrified and fascinated with the graphic details. Who in their right mind would want to be subjected to such a scenario?

On the other hand, she reminded herself, this was just Diana's fantasy. It wasn't like she actually wanted any of that weird, scary stuff to happen in real life. And Callie had to admit, as much as it freaked her out, she admired Diana's forthright honesty. It gave her the courage to admit her own fantasies, though they were far tamer than Diana's.

A few days later, just as Callie had finished

hanging the last picture in her new living room, her phone rang. Diana Johnson flashed across the screen. They had agreed to meet for dinner that evening, and Callie was excited to meet her new friend in person.

"Hello?"

"Callie? Hey there, it's Diana. I just wanted to say hi." The voice on the other end of the phone was high and girlish. There was a sort of odd, metallic quality to her voice, but it was probably just the connection.

"Hi, Diana. What's up? Everything okay?"

"Everything's great. Just thought I'd give you a quick call about tonight. I was wondering, would it be okay with you if my cousin, Damon, were to come along tonight? Remember, I told you about him when we first chatted? He's a really cool guy. I mentioned you to him and he said he'd love to join us."

Callie groaned inwardly, hoping this wasn't going to be some kind of weird match-making type of situation. Having broken up with her boyfriend of four years just before moving to Chicago, she was *so* not interested in hooking up with someone new right now.

"Um," she hedged, trying to think of a polite way to say no.

Perhaps sensing her hesitation, Diana rushed on, "Don't worry, I'm not trying to fix you up or anything." She laughed. "I wouldn't even suggest he join us, except that he offered to take me to this super exclusive, members-only BDSM club after dinner, and I've been dying to go. It's got a real dungeon in it, and he says you can come, too, if you want. Not to mention, he's like this *total* gentleman who always insists on picking up the dinner tab."

Callie felt herself wavering. She'd looked up the restaurant Diana had suggested, and had already decided she could only afford to get an appetizer as her main course, and maybe one drink. But if Mr. Total Gentleman Cousin was going to insist on picking up the bill… Besides, a private BDSM club sounded pretty sweet, and less skeevy than she imagined the public clubs might be.

"Okay," she agreed. She would play it by ear. If things went well over dinner, she might go with them to that cool club. She could just observe. It wasn't like anyone was going to force her to do anything she didn't want to do. "I guess that would be fine. I look forward to meeting you both."

"Great. See you tonight."

After they disconnected, Callie fell back onto the couch and stared at the cell phone in her hand, thinking about tonight. Did she have the nerve to go to a BDSM club with two virtual strangers? Fooling around online was one thing, but to actually go to a dungeon? What if she freaked out or something?

And what did one wear to a BDSM club? Stiletto heels with a leather minidress? She didn't own anything like that. She could at least wear something a little sexy. Not that she had much that could be called sexy. Aside from the tailored suits and dresses she wore for work, she was mainly a flannel shirt and jeans kind of girl. At least, she had been back in Wisconsin.

But this was the new Callie, right? The city girl with a new career as assistant curator at an esteemed Chicago museum. And anyway, she could always take a pass on the club, if it didn't feel right.

Even as she thought this, the idea of going to a bona fide BDSM dungeon sent bubbles of excitement fizzing through her veins. If the vibe felt right, why not? She'd never have the nerve to go to one of those places on her own. This was an ideal way to check out the scene without any risk.

She still had three hours before she had to meet

Diana at the restaurant. Was there time to go shopping for something sexy?

Time, maybe. But money, no. Even with the help her parents had given her, she'd used every bit of her savings to make the move. Until she started the new job at the end of the month, she had no business buying frivolous outfits. If Diana and her cousin arrived at the restaurant decked out in leather gear, so be it.

After trying on various outfits, Callie finally settled on a simple cream-colored button-down blouse tucked into a navy pencil skirt. Examining herself in the mirror, she undid four of the buttons on her blouse to reveal some cleavage. Deciding that was a bit much, she buttoned the blouse again. She didn't want to send the wrong message.

But, wait. These two people she was about to meet were into BDSM. They were sophisticated and comfortable with their sexuality. Why shouldn't she be, too? Lifting her chin, she unbuttoned the blouse again, revealing the tops of her breasts, which were pressed together by the pretty lace pushup bra she wore underneath.

"To the new Callie," she said to her image in the mirror. "Let the adventure begin."

To keep reading Tricked, go to
Amazon.com to get your copy
today!

https://www.amazon.com/dp/B08PW2H3GB

Need something sweeter? Check
out Claire's BDSM romances on
Amazon

https://www.amazon.com/-/e/B001JS32ES

9 7 9 8 7 1 1 9 6 3 4 0 0